PUFFIN BOOKS

Fat Chance

Jacqueline Roy is a lecturer in Black and Women's Literature and
Creative Writing at the Manchester Metropolitan University. Her
books for young adults include *Soul Daddy* and *King Sugar*.

D1434324

Fat Chance

Jacqueline Roy

PUFFIN BOOKS

For my mother,
Yvonne Roy, 1926–1992

PUFFIN BOOKS

Published by the Penguin Group
Penguin Books Ltd, 27 Wrights Lane, London W8 5TZ, England
Penguin Books USA Inc., 375 Hudson Street, New York, New York 10014, USA
Penguin Books Australia Ltd, Ringwood, Victoria, Australia
Penguin Books Canada Ltd, 10 Alcorn Avenue, Toronto, Ontario, Canada M4V 3B2
Penguin Books (NZ) Ltd, 182–190 Wairau Road, Auckland 10, New Zealand

Penguin Books Ltd, Registered Offices: Harmondsworth, Middlesex, England

First published by Blackie 1994
Published in Puffin Books 1995
1 3 5 7 9 10 8 6 4 2

Text copyright © Jacqueline Roy, 1994
All rights reserved

The moral right of the author has been asserted

Made and printed in England by Clays Ltd, St Ives plc

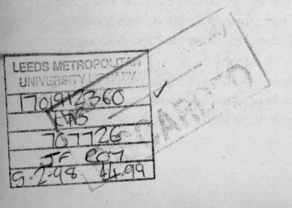

1

Tessa's mother, Joy, squeezed into a pair of size ten jeans and struggled with the zip. Tessa held her breath as she watched, hoping they wouldn't fit. She saw that her mother was holding her breath too as the jeans dug into her narrow waist. The zip slid to a close.

'What do you think?'

'They're OK,' said Tessa, leaning against the wall of the cubicle and observing her mother in the mirror.

'Just OK?'

'Excellent, brilliant, really you, wow, what a fit,' said Tessa in a flat voice.

'It was worth losing those few pounds. It pays to look after yourself.'

'You reckon?'

'I wish you'd try to do something with yourself, love. You could be so pretty, you know that?'

Tessa looked down at her own bulk and felt a stab of disgust. She wasn't even twelve years old, but she weighed a lot more than her mum had ever done. She would barely have got a pair of size ten jeans over one thigh, let alone be prancing about in them looking so happy and pleased with herself.

There was hardly a moment when Tessa didn't wonder what it must be like to be slim. She could picture herself in bright colours: skin-tight leggings and a baggy shirt, oranges and purples and greens, shades that would set off her dark complexion and get her whistles from the boys in her class at school, the kind that Sonia Gordon got. It was the worst luck in the world that Sonia was sitting next to her in class for most lessons. Or maybe it wasn't luck at all, maybe Sonia had planned it that way so that she would look even better than she already did by comparison. Tessa hated Sonia. She was the one who'd hit on the Ten-Ton-Tessie routine. She would. She just would.

'Do you think I should get these then?'

'It's up to you, Mum,' Tessa sighed. They'd been buying something for her mother to wear to the Wedding of the Year, when Tessa's elder sister Hetty would marry Jonathan and they'd sail off together into the sunset. But a mother-of-the-bride outfit hadn't been enough for Joy; it had sparked off a shopping spree. In addition to the dress for the wedding, there were two pencil skirts in a carrier bag, and a dressy top. Now they were going for jeans, and probably a lot more besides.

'Maybe I should try to look more my age,' said Tessa's mother, eyeing her own reflection with a frown.

Tessa sat on the narrow ledge that ran along the cubicle wall. The hardboard sides shuddered dangerously. 'You look all right, Mum.'

'I think your dad would like them.'

'I don't think he'd even notice.' Tessa put her hand to her mouth. She hadn't meant to say that, it had just slipped out. Now that her mum and her father, Paul, weren't together any more, they kept trying to impress each other all the time. Tessa was fed up with it. 'I expect he'll like them,' she said in a low voice, trying to repair the damage.

'Why wouldn't he notice? He's always liked to see a pretty figure. You see some women of my age and they've let themselves go. I've never done that, have I?'

'No.'

Tessa studied the cubicle curtains. What was so terrible about being fat? Did it mean you weren't a human being or something?

'You know, when I was young, really young, I mean, fifteen or sixteen, I was thin as a stick. People used to say I should be a model, but there weren't black girls doing that then, it was before Naomi Campbell. But I could have.'

'Are you going to have those jeans then, Mum?'

'I think so. What do you think?'

'You should,' said Tessa, knowing it was the only way to end this stupid conversation about thinness and being a model.

Joy changed briskly out of the jeans and into her pencil skirt. She looked at herself critically. 'Maybe I could still do with losing a few pounds,' she said.

Tessa fought the urge to say something very rude. She was starting to think that her mother might be anorexic or something. She'd read about it in a magazine; it was this illness where you couldn't stop slimming and no matter how thin you got, you still thought you were fat. Only you were supposed to get it when you were a kid, not when you were coming up to forty. Just her luck to be given an anorexic when mothers were handed out.

'Cash or card?' said the assistant as she pushed the jeans into a carrier bag with 'Dolly' emblazoned all over it.

Joy handed over a card.

Tessa imagined having a credit card of her own, and walking into any shop she pleased and getting whatever she wanted just by presenting it at the till. It would be utterly brilliant. Yet, as she thought about it more, she saw that for her it would be pretty useless really. All she wanted was the kind of clothes she wouldn't fit into in a million years. It didn't matter how much she spent, everything she bought would look ugly as it clung to her ever-ballooning shape. If this was puppy fat, she was the biggest puppy anyone had ever seen.

As they walked down the street, Tessa wondered what people were thinking as they looked at her and her mother. Lots of times they'd been mistaken for sisters, and Joy had given this silly little squeal of false astonishment and had come over all girlish. 'Oh, you're such a smooth talker,' she would say in this excited, breathless voice. 'This is my daughter Tessa, though you know we have been taken for sisters before. I enjoy life and that keeps me young.' It was just gross, and not even true: Joy wasn't a name that suited Tessa's mother at all – she was pretty fed up most of the time.

'Now what about that T-shirt I promised you?'

'I've got enough T-shirts.'

'You're a funny sort of kid, you know that? When I

was your age, I would have given my eye teeth to have people wanting to buy things for me.'

Tessa pictured eye teeth, the large front ones most likely, with a winking eye set right in the centre of each, taking a peek every time you smiled. Her mother went into another shop and Tessa followed gloomily. Joy wasn't about to take no for an answer, and Tessa would be getting that T-shirt whether she wanted it or not. Maybe she wouldn't have to try it on. No one else her age could even come close to filling a bra, but she was flowing out of one.

'Which one do you like? This one's a good colour.' Joy held up a fucshia T-shirt with a bold black flower design on the front.

'Not that one,' said Tessa.

'Why not? It's such a lovely colour.'

'I don't like bright things. If I have to get one, I want it to be black.'

'Young girls don't wear black. It makes them look old before their time.'

'OK, so I'll be fat and old. Good combination. I'd like that.'

'Don't you start talking back at me. Didn't anyone ever tell you sarcasm's the lowest form of wit?'

'No, no one ever mentioned that,' answered Tessa.

Her mother was out of earshot though, pulling each T-shirt hanging on the rack towards her and then pushing it back with an angry little slap.

'I wouldn't mind a navy blue one,' said Tessa, hoping to make peace.

'I'm not sure you deserve one now.'

'Can we go then?'

'What about khaki? That's a good colour, it's not as drab as navy.'

'I think it's drabber.'

'Or you could have rust. That would suit you.'

'It's too bright.'

'Rust isn't a bright colour,' said her mother, laughing.

Tessa smiled back, wishing she could keep up with her mother's changes of mood. 'OK, then, we'll get that.'

'You sure you wouldn't like –'

'I'm sure. Let's pay.'

'I think you should try it on.'

'What size is it?'

'Medium.'

'I want large.'

'Large is man size. You're not that big.'

'Nearly,' said Tessa.

'If you want to be slim, you have to work for it. Nothing don't come for nothing, not in this world.'

Tessa rolled her eyes. The Dieter's Charter, that's what she'd be getting now. All about calories and the importance of will-power and how a minute on the lips meant an inch on the hips. 'I'm OK as I am,' said Tessa stubbornly. She didn't believe it, she was saying it to annoy her mother.

'If you lost just a few pounds, you'd really feel the difference.'

'I'll have the medium shirt. Can we pay now?'

The shop's lights began to blink on and off to tell them it was about to close. Joy carried the T-shirt to the till. 'You can wear it tomorrow with that skirt I got you.'

Tessa nodded. She'd look terrible, but it didn't matter because whatever she wore she looked terrible. Joy gave her the packed shirt. Not as flashy as 'Dolly'; the bag just had 'Modes' scrawled on it.

Tessa swung the carrier bag to and fro and wondered what 'Modes' meant. Her mother's 'Dolly' bag was thick coloured paper, while hers was sweaty plastic. 'Can I go home by bus?'

'Why would you want to do that when I've gone to so much trouble to bring the car?'

'I like buses.' What Tessa really liked was going to the chip shop on the way back and getting a steaming packet of thick-cut chips drenched in vinegar with plenty of salt.

'I don't understand you sometimes, you know that?'

'Yep. You keep telling me.'

'When I was your age, my mother and father would have taken a strap to me for talking back like that.'

Tessa found this hard to believe of her grandparents. She didn't know them that well because they lived in Jamaica, but from what she'd seen of them, they were kind people who would never beat up on a child. She said as much.

'Things were different then, there was more discipline for children, you were expected to jump to it, no questions asked.'

'Grandad says you were always asking questions. And talking back, and nicking things off barrows in the market.'

'Grandad has a long tongue.'

Tessa grinned. 'That's just what he says about you,' she answered, dodging her mother's hand as it shot out to give her a slap. 'See you later then, Mum,' said Tessa, moving down the road before Joy could stop her. She could almost smell those chips now, and practically taste them, melting hotly in her mouth, the salt sharp on her tongue.

'Don't eat anything on the way back,' called Joy. 'You'll spoil your tea.'

'I won't,' lied Tessa, as she headed for the chip shop.

2

Standing outside the church, waiting for the bride, Tessa wondered why she had ever wanted to be a bridesmaid. Every now and then a gust of wind lifted the flimsy skirt of her dress, exposing her chubby brown knees to the view of passers-by. She could just imagine what they were saying to themselves as they saw her waiting there. They'd all be looking at her bulges and wondering why nobody had thought to put her on a diet. She looked like a blancmange in all that pink, she knew she did. Bridesmaids were meant to be graceful, but she was as delicate as a hippopotamus on roller skates.

A few yards away, her cousins Charmaine and Camilla were giggling with their hands over their mouths, and spluttering so-called witticisms at one another about pink elephants. Then they started to imagine being flattened to a pulp when Tessa tripped on the bride's train and landed on top of them half-way up the aisle. Tessa decided that really wasn't such a bad idea, and began to wonder how she could arrange it.

Charmaine was about four feet ten and skinny as a liquorice stick. Her legs were as thin as one of Tessa's arms and she looked depressingly wonderful in a miniature version of Tessa's dress. It was the meanest thing Hetty had ever done, making them wear frilly frocks with high waists. Tessa looked down at her protruding stomach and wondered if people would think she was pregnant.

The bride's car pulled up smoothly beside them and Hetty stepped out, wrapped in yards of lacy white. She was twenty-two years old but she was only a size eight. Her slim ankles were set off by strappy silver shoes, and her veil was the longest Tessa had ever seen, crowned with a garland of roses. Tessa looked at Hetty with a longing so deep it hurt. She would give anything to be so beautiful, anything at all; the god of thinness only had to name it and she would do it if only she could be as beautiful as that.

Tessa stared at her father, Paul, who was holding Hetty's arm ready to escort her into the church. He was wearing a suit he had bought specially for the occasion and he looked like Eddie Murphy, he really did, with hair cut smooth and shiny leather shoes. Tessa felt proud of him. Other people's dads weren't so good-looking, or so tall, and they looked silly in suits, not like him at all.

The photographer took some shots of the arrival and Tessa hastily tried to conceal herself behind Camilla. The cousins had stopped giggling now and were standing to attention like the best little girls in the world.

'I can't see the young lady at the back,' said the photographer. 'Can you come forward a bit, darling?'

Tessa pretended she hadn't heard.

The photographer said, 'Yes, you, the big one. I can't get you in shot. If you'd just stand next to the other one, there's a good girl.'

Tessa peered round Camilla and hoped that this would be enough.

'Hurry up, Tess,' said her father, 'we're waiting on you. We want to go into the church.'

Tessa stood beside the other bridesmaids and tried to picture the end result. Pin-like Charmaine and no-bum Camilla would look truly amazingly wonderful, while she, Tessa, would resemble a circus freak. Come and see the fat lady: only fifty pence.

They began to move into the church, following slowly behind Hetty and Dad. Tessa was out of step. She tried to adjust her pace but she couldn't make it work. She wasn't moving in time to the organ music at all, she was doing it wrong and spoiling things. She felt a flush of embarrassment and knew there were damp patches under her arms, but Camilla and Charmaine continued to look cool in every sense of the word. 'It's not fair,' Tessa muttered to herself, 'it's just not fair.' Heads were turning to look at the small procession and to admire the bride. Tessa's flush deepened. They were staring at her. They were thinking how ugly and stupid she looked.

At the altar, Hetty handed Tessa her bouquet and then turned towards the minister. Tessa relaxed a little. People weren't watching her any more, they were concentrating on Hetty and Jonathan, the bridegroom. Tessa knew she ought to be listening to the words of the service, but there were other things to think about, such as how the chicken vol-au-vents would taste and whether she could prevent people noticing how much she ate.

'Do you, Henrietta Catherine Gloria Hislop, take this man . . .'

Tessa had forgotten that all your names were said at weddings. On her wedding day, she'd be Teresa Jennifer Frances, which wasn't bad, though Jennifer was a bit old-fashioned. Camilla and Charmaine only had one name apiece, so that was something she'd got over them.

Jonathan slid the ring on to Hetty's finger. Tessa wondered if anyone ever had the wrong size ring, and what would have happened if Hetty's finger had been too fat and the ring had stopped at her fingertips, unable to budge any further. If you were too fat for your ring, were you allowed to get married, or did the ceremony have to be stopped? And if they did let you marry anyway, were fat fingers grounds for divorce?

They were kissing now, full on the lips, like they were eating each other. It was sort of nice, sort of embarrassing. Then they moved off into the vestry to sign the register. And then the church part was over and everyone piled out into the sunshine, saying what a lovely wedding it had been and how Hetty had looked so beautiful they'd had to cry. Tessa glanced at her mother; the traces of tears shadowed her cheek. Why did people think so much of weddings? Mostly they ended in divorce, like her mum and dad's had done. It was all a stupid pretence, it didn't really mean anything much.

More pictures. And hell's bloomin' bells, there was someone with a video camera, as if it wasn't bad enough already. Tessa began a flight down the path, out of range of the camera's eye. She sat on a wall at the back of the church, hitching up her dress to do it and wishing she could be more elegant. She was closer to elephant than elegant. Charmaine and Camilla had been right about that, the little . . . Words failed Tessa. You probably shouldn't swear when you were sitting on a church wall, it wouldn't be right, and no other sorts of words were up to the job of describing her cousins. They would be loving the video camera, they'd be practically on top of it, parading their slim little bodies and looking so pleased with themselves, so utterly smug it was enough to make you puke.

Tessa reached into the pocket stitched in the side of her dress and found the eight squares of chocolate she'd hidden there that morning. It was warm and bendy but it hadn't actually melted yet, and the smooth richness filled her mouth so sweetly, it was like all the warm, nice things in the world mixed up and made into something you could eat. If happiness could be turned into something you could see and touch, it would be a chocolate bar, she was sure of it. She screwed the wrapper into a little ball and glanced round furtively. Had anybody seen her eating that? They'd be thinking 'Greedy little pig', and they'd be laughing at her. Nobody had seen it though. They were probably too busy thinking about what they all looked like, and how the photos would turn out.

'Tessa!'

Her mother had noticed she was missing and was sounding cross. Tessa walked slowly towards her, giving the cameras time to disappear. People were getting into

17

cars and heading for the reception. Would there be cake? Wedding cake was OK, but chocolate cake was best, or gâteau, that was good, especially with proper cream.

'Where did you get to?' said Joy.

'Nowhere in particular,' answered Tessa.

'We wanted you in the photos, but it's too late now, they've had to be done without you.'

Tessa hid a smile.

The reception was held in the church hall. It wasn't a sit-down thing, it was a buffet, and Tessa was pleased. At sit-down meals the person next to you, and also the one opposite, could always see exactly what you were eating and how fast you were doing it. This way, you could be on your own most of the time and no one knew if you ate five hundred little biscuits with brown stuff called pâté on them; only she wouldn't want five hundred of those – they weren't that nice, they were actually almost as nasty as they looked, so she moved on to the salmon, which was utterly delicious and took the taste of the pâté out of her mouth.

'All right, Tessa?'

She swallowed a chunk of salmon bridge roll and turned to her father. 'Fine, thanks,' she said.

'Sorry about last weekend, I had to work.'

'It's OK,' said Tessa, though it wasn't. She'd really wanted to see him, and he'd gone off to some conference or other because he'd got the dates mixed up. He was busy all the time; you were when you were a doctor, she knew that, though she sometimes wished it could be different. 'Am I coming to your house at the end of half-term then?' she said.

'You can count on it.'

Tessa nodded, though she knew that in this world you could never count on anything.

'Would you like to bring a friend with you? I may be busy, and it would be nicer for you to have some company.'

'Busy?'

'I'm on call next week.'

'Brilliant.'

'Tessa –'

'It's OK, don't worry about it.'

'Is there a little friend you could bring?'

Tessa thought about the word 'little'. Did her father mean he wanted her to bring someone small and slim? Or was it just a way of speaking? She looked at him questioningly, so he said, 'I have tried to switch so I'm not on call, but there's no one free to cover me. If I do have to go to the hospital, it'll be lonely for you, that's all.'

'There isn't anyone I can bring.' No one except Jasper Woodrow. He was small enough for sure, and ugly with it. Tessa despised him as much as everybody else seemed to despise her, only Jasper never seemed to notice; he trailed after her like a sick dog which made her want to kick him all the more.

'No one?' said her father.

'No one,' repeated Tessa.

'You must have some friends.'

Tessa stayed silent. What was she supposed to say to that? *No, I don't have any friends, everybody hates me?*

19

Sometimes parents were the stupidest people in the entire universe.

'What about school, Tess?'

'What about it?'

'You must have made some friends there.'

'I've only been there three or four weeks, and it's not like juniors, they all like things I don't care about.'

Paul picked a piece of salmon roll from Tessa's plate and dropped it easily into his mouth. He was a large man, Tessa decided, but not fat, not at all. He could probably eat anything he wanted and never put on an ounce. She'd never known him worry about food, he just ate whatever he felt like whenever he wanted to. She wished she took after him.

'What things do they like at school that you're not into?'

'Oh, you know. Clothes. Makeup. Who's going out with who. All that.'

'It's a phase girls go through, but it happens to some sooner than others.'

'It's never going to happen to me.'

Her father smiled in the annoying way grown-ups do when they've decided you've got something wrong and you'll change when you get older. She wasn't going to change, there was no point, not unless she lost three stone or more, and pigs would fly first.

'So you don't want to bring a friend?' repeated Paul.

'I've already said,' Tessa answered crossly.

'Well, it's up to you,' Paul replied, in his best tolerant voice. Tessa knew that now Paul wasn't at home any more, he kept worrying that she wouldn't like him so much. Therefore, however often Tessa provoked him, he still tried to be nice. Only sometimes, it was as if he'd stopped being Dad. He wasn't like a father any more, he was like a friend, but it felt wrong, your dad being your friend, and she wished he'd realize that.

Tessa noticed her mother edging towards them, half-eagerly, half-nervously. Joy wanted to see Paul, but wasn't sure he'd want to see her, Tessa could tell. It was embarrassing, the way grown-ups behaved with each other, they made everything so tangled up. Tessa decided to leave them to it and went to get some cake. Only they'd gone for adult sort of cake like sour lemon cheesecake and some kind of fruit tart, and that wasn't a lot of fun – cakes should be sticky and sickly sweet, she thought everyone knew that. Charmaine and Camilla were eating crisps and drinking lemonade. They picked at their food, even really exciting food, like they didn't really care what they were eating. Tessa wished she didn't care. You could diet so easily if you didn't mind what you ate and if you didn't see the difference between crispbread and chocolate.

Someone was telling them to assemble for speeches. All the eating was meant to be over. Tessa crammed a piece of the grown-up cheesecake into her mouth and found it tasted better than she'd thought it would. She wished she'd left herself time for a second piece. Her father was doing a speech about how lovely Hetty looked and how proud he'd felt when he'd walked her down the aisle. Tessa wondered how he'd feel when her turn came and he was stuck beside a walrus on human legs. She wanted him to be proud of her too, but who could be proud of anyone so disgusting and huge? And then there was Mum. She thought being thin was the most important thing in the whole world, that it mattered more than being good or happy or brave or anything. And maybe she was right, because whoever heard of anyone marrying anybody else because they were *good*? You liked people and went out with people and then married them because of the way they looked, everyone knew that. Tessa ate another piece of cheesecake and resigned herself to loneliness. It wasn't as if she even cared, not really. And she didn't want to get married either, not ever, because weddings were stupid, and so were all the people who went to them, especially the thin ones. It was obvious.

3

Jasper Woodrow was in Tessa's class. His family had come to England from Jamaica so long ago that his parents had been born in London, just as Tessa's had been, but as far as she was concerned, this was all they had in common.

Jasper was the smallest person in Class 7W, and he had such skinny arms and legs that Tessa could picture herself walking up to him and breaking each in two with her bare hands. He wore tortoiseshell-rimmed glasses that had thick lenses. These magnified his insect eyes so that they stared out uncannily from behind the glass. Yet because he was a dreamer, he never quite seemed to focus on you; he was always looking slightly past you into space.

Tessa's greatest pleasure in life was Jasper-baiting. It was so easy, she didn't even have to work at it. He was just made to be laughed at, and every time she laughed at him the fact that the rest of the class was laughing at her was made a little easier to bear. It meant she wasn't the only victim; there was someone else as miserable as she was.

As Tessa walked slowly to school, ignoring the Here-Comes-Ten-Ton-Tessie taunts that filled the air around her, she thought about how she might tease Jasper that particular morning. Not noticing him, no matter what he said or did, was always fun. Or noticing him solely to tell him how ugly he was gave her lots of laughs. Or maybe she should scribble on his English essay before he had a chance to hand it in, the way someone in their class had scribbled on hers the other day. She didn't even have to come up with ideas for baiting old Jasper, she only had to remember the nasty things that had been done to her to hit on some really delicious schemes.

Class 7W was right at the top of the school building, five storeys up. Sonia always ran easily up the stairs, laughing and joking with three or four boys as she went. Tessa struggled. She was just about OK on the first flight, but after that her breath came in pants and a trickle of sweat began to form and slide down the bridge of her nose. No one else in the entire school seemed to sweat as much as she did. They called her smelly sometimes, and she didn't want to believe it, but every now and then she wondered if it might be true. She always wore two coats of deodorant and showered morning and evening, but you could never tell how you smelled to other people and with all that sweating she could easily whiff a bit. It made her cringe inside just to think of it.

Jasper was coming up the stairs behind her. She didn't need to turn around to look, she just knew from the way the steps tapped and faltered, as if the walker wasn't sure where he was going and was fumbling along. Tessa kept her eyes in front of her even when Jasper had caught up and they were moving side by side.

'Hello, Tessa.'

Tessa ignored him. She ignored him every single morning, but he never seemed to take the hint, he always came back for more. If he was so dim and such a glutton for punishment, he deserved everything he got, Tessa decided.

'My Uncle Bob took me to American football at Wembley Stadium on Saturday. They had fireworks at the end, it was excellent.'

Tessa still didn't speak, though it was mainly because they were coming up to flight five and she didn't have the breath to do it.

'I think they should have lifts. Whoever designed this building was pretty thick in my opinion,' said Jasper.

Tessa glared at him. She didn't need sympathy, and coming from him, it was almost insulting. How dare he pity her in any way! If anyone was to be pitied, it was old four-eyes with his buck teeth. She walked slowly to the classroom door, trying to conceal her wheezing. No one else was panting like she was. Sonia called her Bagpipes and rocked with laughter, her entourage rocking with her.

'Skinny!' retorted Tessa, though she wished she could think of something more damaging to say.

Sonia looked pleased. 'You can't be too rich or too thin,' she said.

Tessa looked at her feet. All her jibes at Sonia turned out sounding like compliments. The trouble was, Sonia had it all, looks, friends, a nice home, two parents living happily together. It was hard to find anything mean to say about that.

'Well, Sonia, it's a pity that you were made so thin in the kindness department,' piped Jasper.

Everybody looked at him, falling silent. He could do that, Jasper, he could say really cutting grown-up things. That was why people usually didn't bother trying to make him look small. Yet the funny thing was, he never said sarcastic things to Tessa, even though she baited him so much. He was a weird sort of person, he really was.

'All right 7W, line up quietly please,' said Mrs Frampton, their form teacher.

There was some jostling as everyone found their place in the line. They began to move into the classroom.

Tessa's desk was next to Jasper's, with Sonia on the other side. He always sat next to her in every lesson. She wondered why he couldn't give someone else the pleasure.

Jasper produced a brown paper bag. 'I got this for you, Saturday,' he said. He put it on the desk beside her, looking at her expectantly.

Tessa wanted to say, 'Whatever it is, I'm not interested,' but she couldn't quite bring herself to do it. The bag might contain cake, or a Mars, or some of those chocolate peanuts, perhaps, and Tessa could feel her pulse quickening with anticipation. She prodded the bag, trying to guess, and then pulled out its contents quickly. It was a pencil sharpener in the shape of a brightly-coloured monster, the kind of thing six-year-olds – or Jasper – might like. Tessa fought her disappointment. 'What would I want with that?' she said.

'I thought it might cheer you up,' said Jasper in a small voice.

'Well it doesn't, it depresses the hell out of me, OK?' Tessa tossed it back on his desk. He picked it up slowly and put it in his pocket, with a look of misery on his face that was so intense that Tessa very nearly felt sorry for him.

After assembly on Mondays, they always had maths. Tessa did the examples they'd been set with ease. She enjoyed working out problems. If only real life had such simple solutions. Beside her, Jasper was working at roughly the same pace. They were both good at work, the best in the class. But what was the point of being clever if you looked like the elephant woman? No one liked clever kids anyhow.

After French, there was a break. Tessa unwrapped a Bounty and started to eat it slowly, but then hunger overcame her and she stuffed the second little bar into her mouth whole. At that moment, Sonia came up and said, 'Guzzle, guzzle, guzzle. What a little piglet you are, only fit for a sty. You know what? I can smell you from here.'

Tessa turned her face away and tried to chew without moving her lips. She spluttered, and some of the coconut went down the wrong way. Sonia banged her back with such spiteful force that Tessa thought she was going to fall. She grabbed hold of the wall beside her and grazed her hand in the process.

'Clumsy,' said Sonia, with a graceful flick of her strawberry blonde hair.

Tessa righted herself and nursed her grazed hand. She would have liked to have gone to the sick-room for a bandage and a few words of comfort, but she was afraid that Nurse would think she was clumsy too. Anyway, although it stung it didn't look too bad, and Tessa didn't want anyone to think she was making a fuss about nothing. *Big girls don't cry*, that's what people said. Tessa wished that it was true.

Sonia skipped off to talk to some of the boys. Martin Picard was there, and Tessa watched them sharing licks of a strawberry lollipop. No one ever shared sweets with her, they were afraid she'd wolf the lot. Martin was nice-looking; he had style. He looked like a young American rapper or something. A geometric design was carved delicately along his scalp and his bottle green shirt looked smart against his clear black skin. Tessa sighed.

'Does it hurt?'

Tessa jumped. She hadn't realized Jasper was there. 'Only when I laugh,' she replied.

Jasper grinned. 'I don't like Sonia,' he said.

'You must be the only boy who doesn't.'

'She thinks I'm ugly.'

'She thinks everyone's ugly except her.'

Jasper grinned again. Tessa realized she'd spoken several polite sentences to him and this was not a good idea – it would only encourage him. So she began to walk away towards the football pitch. She looked over her shoulder and saw that Jasper was behind her like a shadow, always the same number of paces back. Didn't he have any pride? Couldn't he see she didn't want him there?

'Get lost, Jasper.'

He gave her his sad look, like she'd just sat on his baby hamster or something. He kept on after her though.

'You should go to Nurse about your hand.'

'It isn't much.'

'It looks quite bad to me.'

'Does it?' Tessa examined the graze again, willing it to look bad enough for sympathetic attention. It was bleeding a little, and the skin around it was bruised.

'I'll go with you, if you want,' said Jasper.

'Will you?' said Tessa. If someone took you to the nurse, it looked far more serious than if you went on your own. Tessa led Jasper into the main school building.

The school nurse was sitting in her little room, writing something on an official-looking piece of paper. 'What's the problem?' she said.

'I've hurt my hand,' said Tessa in a weak little voice, holding it out for inspection.

The nurse dutifully looked. 'Mmmm, that's sore I should think, but it's not too bad, it won't need a dressing, just a bit of a clean.'

Tessa looked disappointed. 'Won't it get better quicker with a plaster on?'

'No, just the opposite. It needs some air.' She looked at Jasper as if she'd only just noticed him standing there. 'What's wrong with you then?'

'Nothing, I came with Tessa.'

'Well, there's nothing you can do here, so why don't

you go back into the playground? You know you're not allowed in.'

'I came with Tessa,' Jasper repeated.

'Well, you're not needed now. Go on, there's still a few minutes left of break.'

Jasper left at the speed of a quarter of a mile an hour. Tessa was pleased. She had the nurse all to herself now. She watched as antiseptic was poured into a silver bowl and braced herself for the sting as it was rubbed around her hand with cotton wool.

'There,' said the nurse.

'There' was nurse talk for it's all over now and she should disappear the way that Jasper had. But Tessa didn't move.

'Is there something else?'

'No,' said Tessa. She couldn't do it. She couldn't ask how people got thin and if diets always worked as long as you stuck to them. Asking would be the same as admitting she was fat and she didn't want to say it, it hurt too much, it was like admitting you stole, or pinched babies.

'Don't forget, give it lots of air. It really doesn't need a plaster.'

'No,' said Tessa. The nurse returned to filling in her form, so Tessa slowly went out into the corridor.

Jasper was waiting for her. 'How was it?'

'Fine.'

'I bet it stung.'

'It did.'

'I had to have stitches once, in my leg. That really stung. I fell off my cousin's bike.'

Tessa didn't want to hear that Jasper's hurts had ever been bigger than her own. 'I got concussion once. Everyone thought I'd fractured my skull and there was buckets of blood.'

'Honest?'

'They nearly had to operate, and if they had, I would have died.'

'Honest?' said Jasper again.

'My dad's a doctor.'

'Honest?'

'Don't you say anything except honest all the time?'

'Does he work in a hospital?'

'Yes, and he lives in a flat opposite, so that he can always be with his patients when they need him.'

'Doesn't he live with you then?'

Tessa felt stupid. She'd given it away. Why couldn't she keep her stupid big fat mouth shut? 'What about your dad?' she countered, hoping to put Jasper off the scent.

'I don't have a dad,' said Jasper. 'I've never had one.'

Tessa didn't want to hear about Jasper's troubles. What was she supposed to say to that? She wished she'd never mentioned it. But Jasper was obviously waiting for some response, so she said, 'Of course you have, everybody has to have one some time or you can't get born,' and immediately wished she hadn't. You weren't supposed to say that, you weren't supposed to say anything because it was embarrassing. She didn't have any social skills at all, she was just a moron.

'I meant I never knew him. My mum's a single parent.'

Tessa wondered why Jasper was talking like a documentary on problem kids. 'It doesn't bother me whether you've got a father or not,' she said.

'It doesn't bother me, either,' said Jasper. 'My mum's great. You don't need two parents all the time, it's a load of rubbish if you ask me. I wouldn't have mentioned it if you hadn't asked. You never told me your dad wasn't at home any more.'

'Why should I?'

'No reason. I just thought you would have said, that's all.'

'He wants to be home with me, it's just his work, it makes him very busy all the time. My mum's a pharmacist, she's just done a degree, at university.'

'How come? Isn't she too old?'

'No, stupid, you can do it any time you want, nobody stops you or anything. Mum says it's the best thing she ever did, only she was always busy, doing essays and stuff, and now she's busy working. Or dieting. She's always on a diet.'

Jasper looked surprised. 'But I've seen your mum. She's thin.'

Tessa began to run awkwardly down the stairs.

Jasper knew he'd said the wrong thing and he was sorry; it had been going so well and then he'd gone and spoilt it. 'Tessa! Wait a bit.' She wasn't waiting. She was going faster and faster, like she was really angry and couldn't bear to be anywhere near him. 'I'm sorry, Tessa,' called Jasper, only he didn't know exactly what he was apologizing for. He increased his own speed. He was quite a good runner when he put his mind to it. He was gaining on her, he could tell. As she turned the corner, he caught up. 'Sorry,' he said again. A heavy silence fell between them. He wanted to break it, but he wasn't sure he wouldn't say the wrong thing again. At last, he said, 'My mother works in a shop.'

'So what? I don't care what your mother does.' Jasper had his squashed hamster look again, so Tessa said, 'Which shop?'

'The delicatessen in the High Street. Would you like to see her? I could show you where she works after school.'

'I'm very busy at the moment.' This was the phrase Tessa's mother used when she got an invite from someone she didn't really want to visit.

'That's all right, I shouldn't have asked really because I'm very busy too.'

Jasper was talking tough, but his face was soft as butter and about to melt into salty tears. He forced them back pathetically. Tessa groaned softly. 'Maybe you could come round to my dad's. He wanted me to bring somebody, only it has to be the weekend after half-term.'

Jasper's face was transformed. 'I'm free that weekend, I'm not busy at all.'

'Good,' said Tessa, meaning the opposite. It was too late now though, she'd asked, and she couldn't take it back, not even under torture or the Spanish Inquisition.

Even Jasper's walk was different now. It was almost skippy, like Sonia's.

'It won't be very interesting,' said Tessa, feeling guilty about suggesting that her father was boring but wanting to curb Jasper's enthusiasm.

'I don't mind,' said Jasper happily.

'I mean, maybe there's somewhere else you'd rather go.'

'No,' said Jasper. 'I'd like to come a lot.'

'He doesn't have a computer, or even a video.'

'We could play games.'

'What games?'

'Dungeons and Dragons. Monopoly. Chess.'

'I can't play chess.'

'I could teach you.'

'It's a boring game.'

'I don't like it much either.'

'You do. You belong to the chess club.'

'Yeah, I know,' said Jasper. 'But I don't really like it. I like Monopoly better.'

'You're a liar.'

'I'm not.'

'You are, a big, rotten stinking liar, Jasper Woodrow.'

'Does that mean I can't come to your dad's house?'

'I'll need to think about it,' Tessa said.

4

Tessa sat on the top deck of the bus and looked down at a girl of eleven or twelve who was standing at the next bus stop. She was wearing a short green skirt with black tights and neat little ankle boots. Whenever Tessa saw a girl of roughly her own age, she assessed her shape, tried to guess what size clothes she wore and proceeded to envy her deeply. This kid was totally enviable. Tessa hadn't yet seen an eleven-year-old who was fatter than she was. She longed for the day.

'Why do we have to go round to Hetty's?' asked Tessa in a tone that her mother usually described as whining.

Joy managed to ignore the tone and said, 'Because it's Hetty's day off work and I thought it would be nice. We haven't had a chance to see her since the honeymoon.'

'Well, why do I have to come then? I've got lots I want to do this half-term. There's a good film on TV this afternoon too. I really wanted to see it.'

Joy gave in to her irritation. 'Stop whining, Tess,' she said.

Tessa leant back in her seat, satisfied that she was behaving badly enough. She wanted to be annoying. That way, her mother would have to think twice about taking her next time a visit to Hetty was planned. This was half-term; she ought to have some say in what she did, whereas her mother still treated her like a baby and decided everything for her.

It wasn't that she didn't want to see her sister, or not exactly. It would be interesting to see the new flat and to guess what it must be like to be grown-up and married to someone like Jonathan. Hetty might even say something about it to Joy if Tessa appeared not to be listening. Tessa had learnt a lot of family secrets by pretending she was deaf to all the things she wasn't meant to hear. You had to be very careful, though. One flicker, and they realized you were listening and shut up immediately or sent you into the garden as if you were two. No, visiting Hetty was all right from that point of view. It was just that Hetty was so utterly beautiful, right size, right shape, and she never ate too much of anything. It made Tessa feel more awkward and fat and clumsy by comparison, and she didn't need it, she really didn't.

'Why couldn't we have waited till the car was fixed? Then we wouldn't have to do this stupid bus journey.' Tessa knew she was pushing her luck, but she couldn't resist an extra go at her mother.

'Tessa, I'm not telling you again. Stop being such a darn little nuisance.'

Tessa went back to looking out of the window. She liked having the word 'little' applied to her.

They got off the bus and walked beside a park. Tessa looked at the children's playground with its swings and tall slide. She used to like swings, when she was at junior school, before she grew too fat to fit her bottom on one comfortably. You were supposed to be under twelve, but even when she was ten the woman in the playground hadn't believed her and hadn't let her go on. It wasn't fair.

'Don't dawdle, Tess, or we'll be late and the food will spoil.'

Tessa wondered what Hetty would cook for them. She usually did something fancy in order to impress them. Joy couldn't cook properly; she was useless. In fact, Tessa sometimes wondered how she'd got so fat with a mother like Joy, who burnt practically everything and made soggy sandwiches for her lunch box. Tessa had begged to go back on school dinners, because her mother's food was so much worse than anything school could come up with. The only thing Joy cooked really well was chocolate cake. No one knew why that turned out OK when everything else she made turned out so badly.

'Here we are,' said Joy, opening an old wooden gate. They went round to the side of the house and rang the doorbell. It was called a garden flat, but it was just a basement really. In the old days, it would have been where the kitchen was, or the cellar or something. It wouldn't have been somebody's house.

Hetty was wearing an apron when she let them in. Her face had smudges of white sauce on it. She kissed Joy and tried to kiss Tessa, but Tessa was too quick for her and ducked aside before it could be managed. Hetty looked offended for a minute, but then she laughed and showed them into the living-room.

Tessa had been determined not to like it, but now she had to admit it was quite pretty. There were cream curtains with rust-coloured flowers at the windows and a rust carpet on the floor. The sofa was cream and there was a table by the wall with a vase of chrysanthemums on it. Even the flowers were rust. Everything was neat and tidy, which was odd, because when she'd been living at home, Hetty had been the untidiest person on this earth, and the room she'd shared with Tessa had always been a tip. It seemed very unfair of her to get tidy now, when she had a place of her own and could be as untidy as she liked. Tessa had wasted so much time arguing about the mess and Hetty had never done anything about it. But now there was nothing out of place. It was absolutely sickening. Tessa turned away from it all in disgust.

'It's very nice,' said Joy, proudly.

'Thanks, Mum,' said Hetty.

'I can't believe I have such a grown-up daughter.'

Tessa made being-sick noises, and they all laughed.

'You're as horrible as ever, Tess,' said Hetty.

'So are you,' Tessa replied. She found her way into the kitchen. This wasn't so tidy, as the preparations for the meal hadn't been cleared up yet. But Tessa could see that normally it must look pretty nice. One of Jonathan's relations was renting it to them at a cheap rate. Hetty had all the luck, she never had to struggle with anything. People even fell over themselves to help her with somewhere to live. But nobody else saw that Hetty was just plain fortunate. They all thought it was through hard work and something she deserved. Tessa wouldn't have minded this, except that Hetty was held up as an example all the time. *If you don't do all your homework, you won't go to university and you won't get a good job like Hetty.* Or, *Hetty never used to talk back like that.* And then there was, *If only you were better behaved. Hetty would never have done that.* It was a miracle Tessa could bear to be in the same room as the wonderful Hetty, she decided. Then she tried to imagine herself at twenty-two or three, living in her own flat. It would be amazingly excellent, like having a huge doll's house all of your own. But she wouldn't have furnishings like Hetty's. She'd have wild colours, reds, yellows and oranges, and a bedroom all in black, like a tomb. She'd decorate the rooms to amaze; she'd have huge metal statues like robots. She'd seen them in Camden Market once. They'd be standing in each corner. And she'd have a juke-box and every time anyone wanted to listen to music, they'd have to put money in, except that it would be free to her. And she'd have a bed with a golden bedcover on it, and the gold strands would be real gold. Only maybe that wouldn't be right with all the starving people in the world. Tessa tried to shut the image of starvation she'd just created from her mind. It made her feel so guilty and sad. Why had she been born in Britain instead of in one of the driest desert parts of Africa, or in a country torn by war and disease? Just luck, or something. It was frightening. Tessa returned her attention to the imaginary room. Cut the gold thread bedspread then. A black cover on her bed would be best, to match the room. She'd have pretend tombstones in it, and models of Frankenstein and Dracula. And if she could get a coffin from somewhere (was it allowed?) she'd have one of those in her bedroom too, but it would be left open and she would display her collection of badges in it. She had nearly a hundred different ones already, and by the time she was twenty-two there would probably be thousands. She'd pin them to the satin bits round the coffin. They would be very eye-catching.

Hetty came in. 'Do you want a drink?' she said.

'Can I have what you're having?'

'Tea? If you want it.'

Tessa didn't really like tea. 'Maybe I'd rather have coffee.'

'I'm not making coffee just for you, Tess. There's some Coke in the fridge.'

Tessa opened the fridge door. It was wonderfully full. There was some kind of flan, with fruit and whipped cream. 'Is that what we're having for pudding?' asked Tessa hopefully.

'Wait and see,' answered Hetty. She was being depressingly grown-up.

They had home-made tomato soup for lunch, followed by chicken pie with vegetables and mashed potatoes. Tessa ate two helpings. Hetty made really good pastry, it melted in the mouth, just like the food programmes said it should. And there was flan for pudding, and it was mega brilliant, Tessa had three bowls of it, and her mother gave her the frown which said 'Don't be such a pig', but how could you help pigging out on such a good flan? It was beyond your capabilities, it really was.

'I'll help you with the washing up,' said Joy, casting a look in Tessa's direction which meant she should at least be offering. Tessa volunteered her services.

'Mum and I will do it,' said Hetty. 'It's easier.'

Tessa protested. 'I won't break anything,' she said.

Joy and Hetty exchanged looks. They were '*What a difficult child*' looks, mixed with a wish not to dwell on the fact that Tessa was always dropping things; she was clumsy and awkward and only kindness was preventing them from mentioning it.

'OK,' said Tessa, before they got any more embarrassed about her. 'I'll listen to my Walkman or something.'

Or something, Tessa decided. It was a good plan, sitting with them in the kitchen and turning on the Walkman so that they thought you weren't listening, but actually having the music on very low so that you could listen without them realizing it.

Hetty said that everything with Jonathan was fine, but she'd decided to make him wash his own smelly socks, she wasn't going to be anyone's slave, those days had gone.

Joy laughed and said if she'd done that from the start with Paul, they might still have been together. Tessa turned the music down so that it was almost non-existent. 'How is Dad?' said Hetty. 'I've spoken to him on the phone, but I haven't seen him.'

'Oh, so-so,' said Joy. 'He's fed up with the hospital, and applying for other posts.'

'What about you, Mum? Still enjoying your work?'

41

'Oh yes, but I wish I had more time.' She gestured towards Tessa and lowered her voice. 'She's being difficult, you know. She has been for months.'

'She didn't like it when you were so busy studying, and she misses Dad – it's understandable.'

'Yes, I know.'

'She's putting on more weight . . .' Tessa turned the volume up as loud as she could without damaging her hearing. She didn't want them to go on about how fat she was and what it was a sign of. She wished she wasn't there. She wished it was *Star Trek* and somebody could beam her up. She went to the bathroom, always a safe place to go when people started talking about you. It was next to the bedroom, and was painted in lilac with black and white tiles round the walls. Tessa couldn't decide if she liked it or not. Her bathroom would have a round bath and a jacuzzi, though she wasn't quite sure what a jacuzzi was. It sounded nice, and special, so it would be a good idea to include one, she decided. And she'd have pictures of sea-horses on the walls and soap in the shape of a sea-horse too. And she'd have big towels with Mickey Mouse on them in red and yellow to brighten things up. Hetty's bathroom was too sensible and boring.

There was cake with coffee in the afternoon. Tessa wondered if she should have any if they were thinking how fat she was, but in the end she couldn't resist and had three pieces. She would have had four, but she was afraid they'd say something if she did.

Jonathan came home shortly after. He was dressed in

his work suit and it made Tessa slightly nervous of him. He didn't seem like a brother-in-law, he seemed like your dad or something. Tessa wasn't sure how she should behave when he was there. It was odd, having someone count as a member of the family when you didn't even know them properly. It made you confused over what you should talk about.

Luckily, Jonathan didn't seem very sure either, and in the end he turned the television on. He and Tessa watched a game show and an Aussie soap while Hetty and Joy went on talking about work and all kinds of other things, only Tessa wasn't really listening to what they were saying, she'd had her fill of that.

They left just before seven. Jonathan offered to drive them home, but Joy said no, they didn't mind getting the bus. Tessa wished her mother wouldn't speak for her as well; she minded getting the bus very much – it was a cold night and starting to rain.

Tessa pulled up the hood of her anorak. Joy walked beside her with dainty steps, her heels tapping out a neat little beat on the pavement. Tessa was half a head shorter than her mother, but twice as fat at least. Joy was wearing a long, dark red raincoat that was pulled in tightly at the waist. She looked so slender and elegant in it. Tessa became self-conscious and fell out of step. It was as if she'd forgotten how to walk properly, and which foot went first and how the other was supposed to follow it.

They waited for the bus to come in an old shelter which leaked. They were standing by a street light, which cast its beam on them like a spotlight. Tessa wished her mother wasn't so thin and pretty-looking. There was nothing worse than having a lovely mother when you were an ugly child.

5

Tessa was dreaming. She was in this pit, being pursued by demons that bore a passing resemblance to her form teacher, Mrs Frampton. Tessa was wearing nothing but a very tight vest and a tiny pair of knickers. The whole class was standing over the pit to watch, and they were laughing till the tears ran down. Every now and then, one of the demons caught her and prodded the wobbling flesh that hung over her underwear with a red hot poker. Tessa shrieked and ran some more, her thighs rubbing painfully together until they were raw. 'You are being punished for your cruelty to Jasper Woodrow,' the demons howled and Tessa saw him leaning over the pit, tears streaming down his face, but his were tears of pain, not laughter, he was hurting as much as she was.

'I'm sorry, Jasper, make them stop!' Tessa shouted in the dream. Only she must have said it out loud, because her mother was shaking her awake and saying it was only a nightmare.

'Oh, Mum,' whimpered Tessa with a little sob.

'It was just a dream. Dreams can't hurt you. Go back to sleep.'

'I'm scared to. There were all these horrible slimy little creatures with green scaly skins and they were chasing me and prodding me with stick.'

'Sounds like a guilty conscience to me.'

45

Tessa pulled the blanket round her uneasily. 'I don't have anything to feel guilty about,' she said.

'Oh, yes, you do,' said one of the demons, who had somehow slipped out of the dream and got inside her head.

'I don't,' she protested. 'I haven't actually told Jasper he can't come on Saturday. I only said I'd have to think about it.'

Her mother sat on her bed. 'It's half past two,' she said. 'I need my beauty sleep now that I'm working again.' Joy was a pharmacist now she'd got her degree. She handed out medicines at a big chemist's shop. But although she protested, she continued to sit on the bed, and she held Tessa's hand. 'Who's Jasper?' she said.

'He's no one, just this kid in my class. Dad wanted me to bring a friend this weekend and I told Jasper he could come, only now I'm not so sure.'

'What's he like?'

'Small and ugly.'

'You shouldn't judge people by appearances, you know, Tess.'

'Why not? You do it all the time. You think unless someone's thin, they aren't worth shoot.'

'I do not, Tessa.'

'You do, you should listen to yourself.'

'Don't start, Tessa. It's way too late for this.'

'Sorry,' said Tessa. Her mother was being nice, holding her hand and everything, and she was messing it up the way she always did.

'Is Jasper a boyfriend?'

'Mum! I'm only eleven!'

'Kids grow up fast these days. I bet there are some girls in your class who are going out with boys.'

Tessa thought of Sonia. 'Maybe,' she said.

'It's not that I approve. You're right, eleven is too young, and I'm glad you've got the sense to see it. I just don't want you to feel you can't tell me about these things, that's all. I hope I'm your friend as well as your mother.'

'Just a mum is fine,' said Tessa. She wished Joy didn't have to try so hard to be young and trendy. She wasn't young any more, so it was stupid to pretend. There was nothing wrong with being older, just as there was nothing wrong with being fat. 'Do you think I should still let him come to Dad's?'

'This Jasper? Why not?'

'I don't know. It's just that he likes me.'

'You are a funny one. Whatever's wrong with being liked?'

'Nobody likes him though.'

'So?'

Tessa couldn't explain. If your only friend was somebody no one else liked, it meant that you couldn't get anyone better, so it made you even more of a failure. If she was Jasper's friend, then Jasper was all she deserved, and that was more depressing somehow than having no friends at all.

'Let him go with you to your dad's, Tess. If no one else likes him, he must be a bit lonely. Have you thought of that?'

'No,' said Tessa. She hadn't wanted to think of it. 'Maybe Dad won't like him.'

'Why shouldn't he?'

'I don't know,' said Tessa. 'So you think I should let him come on Saturday?'

'Tell you what, I'll ring his mum and get it arranged properly, OK?'

'OK,' said Tessa, though it wasn't OK, it wasn't OK at all.

At a quarter to ten on Saturday morning, Tessa was ready and waiting for Jasper. She had her small overnight bag with two packets of chocolate biscuits, a book and her old teddy bear inside. She knew she was too old for the bear, and she abandoned him regularly, but he was a sneaky little creature and he crept back to her every time, refusing to let her dump him. He was a bit like Jasper, really.

Jasper was early. He didn't know how to be late for anything. Sometimes, he actually wanted to be late for something, like a dental appointment or a visit to his least favourite cousin, but that only meant that instead of being too early, he arrived on time. He was a mouse, and he knew it. It was pathetic to be afraid of being late. Everyone else he knew was late all the time.

'Hiya, Tessa,' he said gruffly.

'Hiya,' she returned, looking apprehensively at Jasper's idea of casual clothing. He was wearing his school blazer over a pair of black cord trousers. Nobody even wore their blazer in school, let alone outside it. What was wrong with him?

'This is my mum.'

'Jasper's here!' Tessa yelled to her own mother. It would be best to get the mums together as soon as possible, and then it wouldn't be so awkward, she wouldn't have to try to think of something polite to say to a grown-up. Joy appeared, and the mothers approached each other with wide-mouthed smiles.

'Mrs Woodrow, I'm so pleased to meet you.'

'Me too. But call me Etta.'

'And I'm Joy.'

'It's very good of you to have Jasper like this.'

'Well, it's Tessa's father they're going to visit. I'm just dropping them there in the car.'

'It's nice to think that the kids are making friends.' Jasper's mother lowered her voice, but Jasper and Tessa had no trouble hearing her. 'You know, Jasper isn't happy at that new school. It's too big, and they're not very friendly in his class.'

'I know, Tessa feels the same.'

'Well, at least they've found each other now.'

Tessa and Jasper exchanged embarrassed glances. They didn't want their inadequacies hung out to dry like this; it was terrible the way adults allowed themselves to be so tactless.

'Can I show Jasper my room?'

'Sure, Tess, that's fine. I'll fetch Mrs Woodrow – Etta, I mean – a cup of coffee.'

Tessa led Jasper up the stairs. 'If you want the bathroom, it's there on your left,' she said.

'No, I'm all right,' said Jasper.

49

'This is my room.'

'It's big, isn't it?' Jasper went to the desk. 'You have a computer.'

'Dad got it for me. I've got the new driving game, where you have to knock down all the pedestrians to score hedgehogs. Want to play?'

'Sure.'

Jasper caught on to the game more quickly than Tessa was expecting. She had to work as hard as she could to stay ahead and she barely managed it. 'You're OK at this,' she said, with grudging admiration.

'I really want a computer. Mum says we can't afford one yet, but I'm saving up all my Christmas money. I've got £45.'

'How long will it take?'

Jasper looked glum. 'Another five years, allowing for inflation.'

'If you put the money in a bank, you'd get interest and then the inflation would be taken care of.'

'I don't think I could walk into a bank. I'd feel stupid.'

'No, you wouldn't. Anyhow, your mum could take you.'

'Would you come?'

'I don't know. I'd have to think about it,' said Tess. 'Want another game?' Then Tessa heard Joy calling them both down. 'Too late. Come on, Jasper, we'd better get going.'

It took fifteen minutes to drive to the flat where Tessa's father lived. Joy stopped in the middle of the road. 'Quickly, out you get. There's a car coming up behind us.'

'Aren't you coming in, Mum?'

'Not this time.'

'Oh, Mum!'

'Hurry up, they're hooting at us.'

'Dad would want to see you.'

'Paul hasn't wanted to see me in a long while, you know that, Tess. It's better to admit it.'

'Mum . . .'

'Come on, Tessa, we'd better go.' Jasper got out of the car, pulling Tessa gently after him.

'I wish —'

'Don't, Tess. Go on, off you go. Have a good time, both of you.'

Joy waved and was gone.

'Which block is it?'

'Straight in front. It's near the top, we have to take the lift.' They stood outside Paul's door. They rang the bell twice, and then knocked, but he wasn't answering.

'He said he was on call, that's why he wanted me to bring someone. I suppose there's been an emergency.'

'What sort of emergency?'

'Someone getting very ill at the hospital. They ring Dad and he has to go.'

'How long will it take?'

'Could be any time.'

'Should we wait?'

'There's a park up the road. We could go there.'

'Will your dad mind?'

51

'Too bad if he does. I mean, what else are we supposed to do, just sit here outside the door waiting for him? Come on, let's go.'

'Will it be all right?'

'Come on, Jasper, stop being so pathetic.'

It was a sunny day, though not very warm. Jasper wished he'd worn his jacket with the hood, not his blazer. The trouble was, because he was so small, he could only wear clothes for seven- or eight-year-olds, and the jacket had a stupid cartoon dog motif on the back, which was totally embarrassing. It was better to wear your school blazer than to be seen dead in that jacket. Anyway, Tessa would have laughed her head off, and he couldn't have borne that.

They walked towards the duck pond. 'You can take rowing boats out in summer,' Tessa said.

'Have you ever done it?'

'Of course I have, lots of times.'

'Can you swim?'

'I don't like swimming,' Tessa answered crossly. She would never, ever let anyone see her in a swimsuit, it was absolutely out of the question. If that meant she couldn't go swimming, then so be it. Trust stupid old Jasper to ask that one. He was a real thicko.

'Do you like swings?'

'We're too old.'

'I'm not. Everyone thinks I'm eight or nine, so no one ever stops me. Will you give me a push?'

'No.'

'Why won't you?'

'Because someone from school might see. They think we're bad enough as it is.'

'I suppose you're right. I keep forgetting you have to behave right for people to be nice to you. At junior school, it never seemed like that, or not so much. People didn't pick on you like they do now, they let you alone more. Now, everybody has to be the same as everybody else, and if you're not, they hate you.'

This was the longest speech Tessa had ever heard Jasper make, and there was some sense to it too. 'I wish I was still in the juniors,' said Tessa. 'The teachers were nicer as well. Now they shout all the time.'

'My mum said we just need to get used to it.'

'We've been there for half a term, that should be enough time to get used to anything.'

'She said maybe we won't get used to it until next year.'

They fell silent at the awful thought of a whole year of being miserable. 'We could be dead by then,' said Tessa, but the thought didn't depress her. At least if you were dead, no one could call you fat guts or golly or chocolate face or ask why you hadn't done your homework. 'What time is it?'

'Half past eleven.'

'Nearly dinner time,' said Tessa.

'What will we have to eat?'

'If my dad's back, he'll do egg and chips or something. Then tonight, we'll phone for a takeaway. It's really good because we have it watching telly and Dad lights candles.'

'What sort of food do you have?'

'Pizza or Indian because they'll deliver those.'

'I don't like pizza,' said Jasper.

Tessa looked at him incredulously. 'You don't like pizza?' she said.

'It's got cooked cheese. I can't eat cooked cheese.'

'But it's . . .' Tessa couldn't find the words to describe the pleasure that eating pizza gave her. How could anyone not like it? Jasper was seeming more than just a little strange, he was practically a head case. It was like he was made all wrong, different from anyone you ever knew. 'I suppose we'll have to get Indian then,' said Tessa after a lengthy silence.

'When are we going back?'

'Not yet. There's a shop just a little way up that hill. It sells ice cream. Do you want one?'

Jasper shook his head.

'I'll buy it for you.'

'No, if I have something now, I won't want dinner.'

'*Honestly?*'

Jasper nodded sadly. He never ate very much, and he was slow at it too. Tessa would think he was pathetic. She thought it already, he could tell.

They went up the hill, Tessa panting and trying not to let it show. They got most of the way up before they realized that the café was closed for the winter.

'It's not fair!' Tessa shouted. 'I wanted a strawberry ice cream and it's shut.'

'We could get one somewhere else, I expect.'

'I wanted one now,' cried Tessa, stamping her foot.

She was behaving like a toddler, and she knew it, but she didn't know how to stop. Every little thing mattered so much these days, especially when it came to food. She'd been looking forward to that ice cream, and she knew it was silly, but not having it after all that anticipation was really hard to bear.

'It's only an ice cream, Tess.'

'You would say that,' said Tessa furiously. 'You don't understand anything, you're just a stupid little . . . squit.'

Squit. It was a lovely word. Tessa's grandmother on her father's side always said it and it snapped off the tongue.

Jasper didn't know exactly what a squit was, but he could tell how nasty it was from the way Tessa spat the word at him. He decided it was best to stay silent until she got over her disappointment about the ice cream. He knew what disappointment was like. One of his uncles had once promised him a visit to the fun fair, only when they got there, they found it had already packed up and gone. Tessa was feeling that same sick sort of feeling he'd had then, it was obvious. The only thing he didn't understand was why she was feeling it about a little ice cream. 'Can we go back now?' he said after a while.

'Yeah, I suppose we ought to,' Tessa replied. She picked a fat blade of grass. 'Can you make it whistle? I can.'

'How?' said Jasper.

'Like this,' said Tessa, placing it carefully between her two thumbs and blowing gently.

Jasper picked some grass for himself. 'I hope a dog hasn't done anything on this,' he said, as he put it to his lips. At first, nothing happened. His cheeks hurt with the effort of blowing. And then a little squeak came out, and then a hoot, and then another, louder and longer than the last. 'I can do it!' Jasper shrieked.

'Blimey, it doesn't take much to make you happy, does it?' said Tessa, but there was more affection in her voice than scorn.

They walked towards the park gates. Someone had painted NO BLACKS HERE on the fence. Jasper stared at it. He looked sad.

Tessa said, 'My dad reckons only stupid people think like that. If you mind about it, you're letting them hurt you, and that's what they want.'

Jasper nodded, making Tessa feel she wanted to protect him. After all, they were in the same boat. They didn't fit, not in any way. Their skins were black, and she was too fat, and he was too wimpy and thin. Nobody liked them, so maybe they should like each other. 'Come on, Jasper, we'd better head back,' she said, and Jasper followed slowly, still tooting on his blade of grass.

6

As soon as they began walking along the corridor towards Tessa's dad's flat, they knew something was up. Tessa slowed down, guessing from the way Paul was standing with his arms folded, glaring at them, that trouble was on its way. Jasper's steps became faltering. Tessa knew that he would be off and running if he could. She wanted to reassure him but there wasn't any point. They were in trouble and there was no way out of it.

'Where on earth have you been?' demanded Paul. 'Get on in here at once!'

'No need to lose your cool,' said Tessa in her most defiant voice. She was scared, but she saw no reason to let anyone know it.

'I've been worried half to death. I even phoned your mother.'

'We went to the park,' said Tessa, sitting on the sofa and pulling Jasper down beside her.

'You went to the park?' her father repeated, as if he could hardly believe the stupidity of it.

'You weren't here. You said you'd be on call, so we didn't know how long we'd have to wait. We thought it was better to do something with our time rather than wasting it standing outside your door.'

'I went to get a loaf of bread, that's all. I was gone ten minutes, max.'

'How were we supposed to know that?'

'Sorry,' mumbled Jasper.

'What?' said Paul.

'Sorry,' Jasper repeated.

'This is my friend. His name's Jasper. I told him it would be all right for us to go to the park.'

'You should have had more common sense.'

'Come on, Dad, we didn't know you'd only gone shopping. It was common sense that told me it would be stupid to hang around here if you were at the hospital.'

'You're getting rude, Tessa, and I won't have it. Your mother may not mind how you behave, but I do.'

'If you really minded, you'd be at home to stop it, wouldn't you?' Tessa muttered under her breath. She could tell by his face that Paul had heard. He looked sad and angry and hurt all at once. 'Sorry, Dad,' she said.

There was a long silence. Then Paul seemed to get tired of the fight. 'Would you two like something to drink? Coke? Orange juice?' he said, in a kinder voice.

'Coke, please, with lots of ice.'

'Jasper?'

'Same, please.' As Tessa's father went to fetch the drinks, Jasper tried not to panic about having to spend two days in a place where people were going to be shouting at each other all the time. As if she read his thoughts, Tessa said, 'It's all right, it's over now. He won't be angry any more. He blows his top, but then he forgets about it. You needn't worry, honest.'

'I don't like Coke, it gives me wind,' Jasper whispered.

'Why did you ask for it then?'

'Because you did, and I thought he was still cross.'

Tessa rolled her eyes and went after her father in the kitchen. It was very small; there was only room for a sink, a fridge, and a little table. There was a cupboard on the wall.

'Dad, Jasper doesn't want Coke. Can he have orange juice?' Tessa opened the fridge door and found the carton. 'I'm sorry we went to the park. I didn't think you'd mind. I wasn't expecting you to worry about where we were and everything.'

'It's all right. I was scared something had happened to you, that's all.'

Tessa saw that if he was worried, it probably meant he cared. This was such a good sign that she felt all bubbly inside and started to giggle for no reason at all.

'What's amusing you?'

'Nothing,' she said.

'Take this in to Jasper then. He must be thinking he's walked into a madhouse.'

Jasper was sitting more or less as Tessa had left him. He might have been a doll, the kind Tessa had read about in stories when she was small. They did nothing when you were watching but they had a great time once you were asleep. Tessa liked to think that Jasper got up to all sorts of things when no one was looking. Life would be very dull indeed for him if he didn't. She handed him his orange drink and went back for her Coke, watching him secretly and hoping he would do something once she appeared to have gone. But he didn't even pick up his glass.

'Is he in your class at school?' asked Paul.

'Yes,' answered Tessa.

'I've never known you to have a quiet friend before.'

Beggars can't be choosers, Tessa thought, but she didn't say it.

'I'd better phone Joy, tell her you've arrived safely. She said you'd have gone off somewhere. Why don't you make some beans on toast? We'll have that for lunch. Get Jasper to help. It might make him feel more at home.'

Making toast didn't seem to make Jasper feel more at home at all. He kept asking whether the slices were done enough and if he should spread more butter on the bread. He seemed to be scared of doing things wrong all the time, and if Tessa hadn't known better she'd have thought he was stupid, really stupid, and not just awkward and shy. Paul seemed to like him though. He told him to go and sit down and watch TV; there was a film on he might like. It was *Gremlins*, and Jasper did like it, and Tessa did too, it was scary and funny and the gremlins were excellent.

'The best bit was when they were watching *Snow White*, and their heads were nodding in time to the music,' Jasper decided.

'I liked the bit where they were in that bar and doing all those bad things,' said Tessa, laughing at the memory. 'Do you want some chocolate? There's some in the fridge.'

They shared a bar of fruit and nut, and Jasper tried not to notice that Tessa ate most of it. He wasn't really hungry anyway, so it didn't matter if he didn't get that much.

The phone rang and Paul had to rush over the road to the hospital. 'I shouldn't be gone long,' he said. 'If there's anything you need, knock next door. It's Greg's flat and he said he'd keep an eye on you, so mind you behave.'

Tessa wished there were more opportunities for misbehaving in her dad's flat, but it was so small, you really couldn't get up to much. 'Are you bored?' she asked Jasper.

'No,' he answered in genuine surprise. 'Why should I be bored?'

'There's not much to do here, and we can't even go out.'

'I don't mind. We could play cards.'

'For money?'

Jasper sounded shocked. 'No! For fun.'

'Cards is boring.'

'There's another film in a minute.'

'You can watch if you like.'

'Not if you don't want to.'

'You don't have to do everything I do all the time.'

'I wasn't,' said Jasper.

'You would if I let you,' answered Tessa. 'OK then, we'll play cards, if you want.'

Jasper cut and dealt like he really knew what he was doing, and as the game of rummy progressed, Tessa realized he was a pretty sharp player and was glad he'd vetoed the money idea. She'd be skint by now if he hadn't.

'How did you get to be so good?'

'I play with my mum.'

'Do you have any brothers and sisters?'

'No, it's just me.'

'I've got a sister, but she's ten years older, so it's like being the only one. She got married a while ago, I think I told you. She went to Jamaica on her honeymoon. My grandparents live there.'

'My grandparents live in Jamaica. You know, I wish I had a sister.'

'Hetty's all right, but she thinks she can boss me all the time. And she's thin.'

'I've got lots of cousins. They're almost like brothers and sisters, and they live close. There's one called Louis, and I don't like him, but the rest are fine, they like to do fun things, swimming and biking and sometimes we go bowling with the uncles.'

Swimming again. Jasper seemed to like it. She could never really care about a person who thought it was fun to prance around in water with practically nothing on. She went into the kitchen and found a packet of popcorn, which she poured into a bowl. 'It's nicer fresh, but Dad doesn't have a microwave. Help yourself,' she said.

Jasper was starting to learn that if you didn't dig in when food was on offer, you ended up not eating, so he took a handful of popcorn and shovelled it into his mouth the way Tessa was doing. 'Have you got Monopoly? We could play that now.'

'OK,' said Tessa, tired of being beaten at cards. She

found the board and assumed she was banker. She began to dole out hard cash. As the game went on, she realized that she was going to win easily. There was no killer instinct in Jasper. He just wasn't tough enough. While she'd demand payment to the last penny, he only said, 'That's OK, pay me when you've got it.' It was kind of sweet, but not how you got to own hotels in Mayfair. She cleaned up, taking everything he'd got. It was a good feeling.

'Do you want to play again?' said Jasper. He didn't seem to mind losing at all.

'OK,' answered Tessa. 'You can be banker this time if you want.'

'What do you think of the kids in our class?' asked Jasper, considering whether he wanted to buy Marylebone Station and deciding against it.

'Some are OK. You know how I feel about Sonia,' sighed Tessa.

'She's a cow,' said Jasper firmly.

It was odd to hear him speaking so forcefully about anyone. 'I think Martin's nice though.'

'He lets Sonia lead him into everything. He doesn't have a mind of his own.'

Tessa considered this. It was pretty accurate. 'Who do you like?'

'I like most people. They just don't seem to like me.'

Jasper managed to say this without feeling sorry for himself. It was a statement of fact, so Tessa didn't think it was worth contradicting it.

He went on: 'I think we should start a club for people

who aren't liked by the majority. We could call it the Oddballs Club, or the Society for People Everybody Hates.'

Tessa laughed. 'Yeah, I'd join. Who needs to be liked anyhow?'

'We could have badges. It could be pretty exclusive. I mean, you'd have to be really hated before you'd be allowed to join.'

'Yeah, and you know what would happen? All the kids would start trying not to be liked and begging us to let them be members of our exclusive club.'

'We could design T-shirts. They could have pictures of wimps on.'

'Or fat girls.'

'Kids with glasses,' shouted Jasper.

'Kids with acne!'

'Black kids.'

'Jewish kids.'

'Kids with runny noses,' said Jasper, pretending to wipe his nose with the back of his sleeve.

'Cross-eyed kids,' said Tessa, looking at her nose and feeling her pupils moving towards it.

'Smelly kids!' said Jasper, sniffing his armpits. 'You know what? I could fit nearly every category. I'd have to be chief member.'

'I bet I could cover more categories than you.'

'No, you couldn't.'

'Betcha I could. Anyhow, I'm bigger than you, I could beat you up and then I'd have to be chief.'

'No,' said Jasper, suddenly serious. 'That wouldn't be

allowed. If everybody hated us, we'd have to be nice to each other, that would be the only rule.'

Tessa fell silent, remembering that this was more or less what she'd decided in the park. Then she said, 'No, there'd be two rules. Being nice, and eating half a pound of chocolate every day. Otherwise, you might lose your acne and your fat and people might get to like you. Then you'd have to leave the club, and no one would ever want to do that because it would be such a good club to be in.'

'You're right,' said Jasper, laughing with her. 'Let's do it, Tess.'

'Yeah,' she said, though she knew they never would.

As if he knew what she was thinking, Jasper said, 'OK, maybe we can't have a big club. But we could have a small one, with just me and you for members, couldn't we? I mean, why not?'

Tessa knew there had to be a reason, but just then, she couldn't think what it was. And at that moment, Paul came in, and the time for telling Jasper that a club for two was out of the question had gone. Tessa was surprised to find that she wasn't sorry about this. What was so bad about Jasper anyway? He was kind, and he made her laugh, and his family had come from Jamaica just as hers had done. Altogether, it was quite a lot to build a friendship on.

7

Tessa was perched on one of the high stools in the lab, and it was wobbling precariously under her weight. Jasper was concentrating hard on the glowing substance in the test tube. It was slowly turning green.

'See? It works,' said Tessa. 'I told you it would.'

Jasper grinned and gave her shoulder a friendly punch, as if to say well done. He liked working with Tessa, she always knew how to go about things, and her ideas were mostly pretty good too.

It was more than three weeks since he'd gone to the flat for the weekend and he still couldn't stop thinking about it. At first, it had been awkward, and he'd felt as if they hadn't really wanted him there. That had been hard, and he'd wanted to go home. But then, after a bit, he and Tessa had begun to realize that they enjoyed the same things and found the same things funny. He even managed to make Tess laugh a few times, and suddenly they were friends, and it was as if it had always been like that. Now, being without Tess was unthinkable. Even school was bearable. Sometimes, with Tessa to share things with, school was almost fun.

'Jasper, you haven't got your mind on what you're doing. You'll spill that in a minute.'

Jasper jumped at the sound of Mrs Frampton's voice. Then he realized it was only Tessa pretending to be Mrs

Frampton, and that the real thing was on the other side of the room. 'That was mean,' said Jasper, but he was laughing. Tessa could mimic practically anyone, she was really clever sometimes. They were always laughing about things now. 'What's next lesson, Tess?'

'Maths.'

Jasper was good at maths, but he didn't really enjoy it, whereas it was Tessa's favourite lesson. She understood sums and problems and equations because, she said, they had a sense all of their own. Writing was harder, there weren't so many rules to guide you and you had to make things up. Jasper enjoyed using his imagination, he didn't understand how anyone could find it difficult. Tessa had tried to explain that she didn't like writing stories or English essays because there was no way of knowing when they were right. Jasper had smiled and said that was the whole point, writing wasn't as right or wrong as maths, and that was why it was interesting. Tessa had sighed, and Jasper had known that she just didn't get it.

Jasper kept wanting to tell Tessa how much he liked her dad, and how he hoped she'd ask him to the flat again, but he couldn't say it in case she laughed about it or made it clear in some other way that she didn't want him there. Jasper had even liked the curry they'd had delivered from the Indian restaurant, and usually he didn't like hot food. That night he'd slept on a mattress in the sitting-room, and he'd felt safe and contented even though he didn't enjoy sleeping in unfamiliar surroundings as a rule. And next day, when Paul had stopped being on call, they'd gone to a performance of African dance. All the dancers had worn vivid costumes in reds and oranges and brightest green, and the music had been so easy to get into, he'd wanted to jump up and dance himself. It had meant a lot because all the men and women in it had been black, and that didn't often happen when you went out to see something in England. It had made him feel proud, although he wasn't sure why. Tessa had loved it too. She'd watched with all her attention and had noticed things no one else had noticed, like the way the smallest dancer moved and the carvings on some of the drums. She was observant, Tessa was. When you went out with her, she showed you things you never would have seen with anybody else.

'Time to pack up now, 7W,' said Mrs Frampton.

Jasper closed his notebook and gathered up his pencils. Tessa had already seen to hers.

'For homework, I want you to write up the notes I gave you. Tessa Hislop, I have a message for you from Miss Jenkins. She asked me to make it clear to you that if you forget your PE kit once more this term, you'll be doing games in your vest and knickers.'

There was a great guffaw from the class. They'd love to see it.

'I couldn't –' Tess began.

'Well, the remedy is in your own hands, isn't it? No one else forgets it's games day as often as you seem to, Tessa, and it's time you were made to remember.'

Tessa fumbled with her pencil case in order to lose the sense that everyone was watching her. She'd known something like this would happen sooner or later. It was bad enough to have to wear one of those stupid, short pleated skirts. That was why she forgot her kit accidentally on purpose each time, so that no one would see her bra and its contents in the changing-room, and stare at her wobbling thighs. Now she'd have to get changed twice a week and in public too, with all the other girls watching and Sonia giving a run-down on the unveiling of the elephant, the way she'd done that first week of term when they'd all been new to the school. It had been the worst day of Tessa's life. The idea of repeating it filled her with sick horror. She'd have to be away, that was the only answer. There was no way in hell that she would go through that again, even if they threatened her with all the punishments in the entire world.

'Off you go then, everyone,' said Mrs Frampton.

Jasper and Tessa trailed out of the lab, last as usual. As they went, Sonia jostled them. 'Fattypuffs and Thinifers,' she said.

'What?' said Jasper.

'It's a story for kids,' said Tessa. 'Trust her to think of that one.'

Jasper didn't mind what they called him. It was different now that he had a friend to share it with. Tessa looked angry and miserable though. 'Just ignore her,' Jasper said.

'I try, but it gets on my nerves.'

'That's what she wants. If you stopped minding, it would take all the fun out of it for her.'

Tessa could see the sense in this, but she couldn't stop

herself minding. The words were like little poisoned arrows that buried themselves just under her skin and seeped their toxins into her, no matter what she did. 'I hate her,' Tessa said.

Jasper drew in his breath sharply. 'It's wrong to hate people.'

'I don't care, I do hate her, and I don't see why I shouldn't. You're such a prig sometimes, you're just too good to be true. Little Saint Jasper, his holiness.'

'I am not.'

'You are. Sometimes I wonder how I can stand you.'

Jasper slowed down so that he was barely moving. That was the trouble with the likes of Sonia, they made everything horrible. But then Tessa was beside him, whispering that she was sorry and she hadn't meant to say that, she'd just been angry, and Jasper was smiling again, and walking as if he could hardly wait to get to the maths class.

At dinner time, Tessa and Jasper lined up together as they usually did. Tessa eyed the trays of chips and sausages and peas and baked beans with hungry eagerness. 'Don't forget to ask for extra chips,' said Tessa. 'Then I can have them.'

Jasper nodded. One of the dinner ladies was his mother's friend, and she thought he needed fattening up. She'd give him extra everything any time he wanted it, and Tessa took full advantage.

'I wish it was fish.'

'I don't like fish,' said Jasper.

'You don't like anything.'

'I do. I like roast potatoes. And apple pie without custard.'

'Is that it?'

'That's it for school dinners. There are lots of home things that I like.'

'No wonder you never put on any weight,' said Tessa, sadly. 'It's jam sponge for pudding. If you don't want yours, can I have it?'

Jasper had forgotten to put jam sponge on his list of likes. 'I do want it,' he said hastily. He knew that Tessa wouldn't really mind because she was fair and it was his pudding. Besides, it wasn't a good idea to behave like a doormat where she was concerned. She didn't like people saying yes all the time, she thought it was boring. Jasper was desperate to keep her interested. Now that he had someone to be with, nothing really frightened him any more. He couldn't even bear to think about how lonely he had been before Tessa had become his friend.

Tessa and Jasper sat on their own at a small table with a smooth plastic top. Jasper fingered the surface. It had been wiped with a damp cloth and the smear marks were visible. Jasper liked things to be perfect. Disorder made him uneasy. And yet, he didn't mind the chaos Tessa brought to everything. That was fun. It was really exciting because you never knew what was going to happen next. One minute she'd be kind to you, the next she'd be yelling at you. At first, he'd been afraid of her changeability, but now he thought it was one of the things he liked best about her. She was different, there was no one else in the world quite like her.

'What are you thinking about?' asked Tessa through a mouthful of extra chips.

'Nothing,' said Jasper.

'You look like you're thinking about something nice. It's mean of you not to share it.'

Jasper merely smiled at her, and swallowed a mouthful of beans.

Late that afternoon, Tessa and Jasper were dawdling along the corridor towards the cloakroom, trying to decide what they would write about for English homework. The class was reading a book called *Sweet Whispers, Brother Rush*, and Jasper thought it was brilliant.

'But it's so sad,' said Tessa.

'Not all through. It's funny as well, like when that nasty woman sees the ghost.'

'The funny parts are fine, and I do like it in some ways. But I hate reading books that make me want to cry. I don't see why things should be sad.'

'But things are sad.'

'I know they are, that's the trouble. I read books when I'm miserable in order to be cheered up. I don't expect the books to be sad as well.'

Jasper struggled to find the words to explain his feelings about sad books. 'But don't they make you feel better because someone else understands what it's like to be miserable? I mean, it makes you feel not alone any more. That's what I want to put in my essay. Don't you see, Tessa? It's a bit like us. We got to be friends because we were both sad.'

Jasper could tell from Tessa's expression that he'd

said the wrong thing. 'I wasn't sad,' she protested hotly. 'Anyway, why do you have to keep talking about how you feel all the time? You're like a bleating sheep.'

Jasper followed Tessa silently down the long corridor. Then suddenly, he let out a long, loud sound: 'Baaaaaaaa.'

Tessa burst out laughing, and Jasper joined in, fizzing up inside with the pleasure of having amused her. 'Fool!' she said, letting her arm rest on his shoulder for a moment. 'Come on, let's get out of this dump. I'll race you to the chip shop.'

Jasper snatched his jacket off the peg and began a slow run, knowing that Tessa would beat him easily just by walking. That was why he needed a head start. You had to be on your toes with Tessa.

8

In Tessa's opinion, there was nothing worse than standing about in the playground on a cold day. Jasper was clutching his chest with his arms in an effort to keep warm. The wind was piercing, and every now and then a flurry of snowflakes fluttered round them.

'I wish it would snow properly,' said Jasper. 'Then we'd have to go indoors.'

'We should be so lucky,' Tessa replied despondently. 'It won't snow until we're back home, and then it will have cleared up by tomorrow morning just so we can get back to school again.'

Mrs Frampton walked briskly towards them in a heavy black coat and warm-lined boots. She was wearing a hood.

'Just like Dracula,' Tessa whispered, and Jasper had to agree.

'Now come along, you two,' Mrs Frampton barked. 'Of course you'll be cold if you just stand about like that. What about a little exercise?'

Tessa glared moodily. Why couldn't teachers just leave you alone? After all, it was no skin off their noses if you froze to death in a playground wilderness. 'I haven't got a ball,' said Tessa hopefully, as if this was likely to free her of all obligation to do exercise of any kind.

'Now come on, Tessa, you and Jasper have a little run. Go as far as the playing field and back, go on. That will warm you up, Jasper, you look like an ice block. I'm not going to have your parents complaining to me that you caught flu in your lunch break just because you stood around like twerps. Off you go!'

There didn't seem to be a choice. Tessa and Jasper set off at a slow jog, knowing that it probably wouldn't make them any warmer, but it would make them look darn stupid. Tessa glanced back, and of course Mrs Frampton was watching and nodding encouragingly every now and then from beneath the hood of her Dracula coat. Tessa had barely gone a few yards, but already she was winded. She slowed to a semi-walk and Jasper followed suit.

Mrs Frampton's voice rang out: 'Faster now, or you won't get warm!' Tessa tried to look as though she were jogging without actually increasing her pace. She swung her arms more and lifted her knees slightly higher. The effect made Jasper splutter.

'Don't laugh, you look just as bloomin' ridiculous, believe me, Jasper Woodrow.'

This only made Jasper giggle even more.

'This is so stupid,' Tessa said. The playing field was still a good way off. She didn't see how she was going to make it. 'Have a look, Jasper. Is Drac still watching?'

Jasper turned his head slightly and then nodded. Tessa gritted her teeth and carried on.

'There's Sonia and Martin,' said Jasper.

'Where?'

'Near the playing field, I can see them.'

'I thought your eyesight was meant to be bad.'

'You can tell Sonia and Martin by the way they stand – sort of tall, with their chests stuck out, as if they're geared up for a fight.'

Tessa nodded, admiring Jasper's powers of observation. It was true, they did stand like that, she hadn't noticed it before. It was obvious that they wouldn't be able to resist having a go as she and Jasper exercised towards them. Tessa tried to decide if she should speed up or slow down as she drew alongside. Speed up seemed best – then they might be past before Sonia could think of anything disparaging to say.

But no; it seemed that Sonia couldn't resist throwing out a snide remark. 'Look at old fat guts puffing past. I'm glad I don't look like that, all lumpy like a great old sofa.'

Martin grinned; he didn't seem to know what else to do.

'I'd never want to look like you in a million years, Sonia Gordon,' Tessa replied, lying through her teeth.

Tessa had slowed to a halt. Sonia looked her up and down and said, 'That's all right then, you've got your wish,' and then that loud laugh of hers rang out across the playing field.

'I hate you, Sonia,' said Tessa in an undertone.

This time, Jasper didn't seem to find this unreasonable. 'Me too,' he said.

Tessa was part pleased, part worried by this response. What if she'd led Jasper into bad ways? He used to be so gentle, and now he was sounding fierce. It seemed wrong, somehow. 'You don't have to hate her as well,' Tessa said. 'I've got quite enough hatred for both of us.'

'Look at them,' said Sonia. 'No wonder they have to go around with each other. No one else will have them.'

'That's everybody else's loss,' said Jasper.

Tessa gave him an encouraging look. They were standing still now and Tessa was trying to get her breath back. She hated having an argument while wheezing; it put you at a terrible disadvantage. 'Anyway,' she said, gulping air, 'at least I get ten out of ten for maths and science. You've never got ten marks for anything in your entire life. I'd rather be fat than stupid.'

This seemed a more effective shot. Sonia actually looked slightly ashamed. She rallied though. 'Who needs clever girls? You can get ten out of ten all you like, but nobody will ever fall in love with you or think you're anything special.'

'Looks aren't everything,' said Tessa, aware that she was sounding like a teacher or a parent.

'At least I've got fair hair, not that stupid wool that you've got on your head,' was Sonia's next response.

Without thinking about it, Martin reached up and touched his own hair uncertainly. It was just like Tessa's and Jasper's and he wasn't sure he liked the way the argument was going. 'Come on, Sonia,' he said. 'There's a good footy match over there. Let's play. It's better than freezing here.'

Sonia just ignored him. She was having too much fun. 'Ever thought what old fat guts would look like in her games kit, kicking a ball around? I think I'd like to see it. Those fat brown knees bulging over football socks would be such a treat to look at. And then there's Jasper, a.k.a. Bauble Eyes. They make such a lovely couple.'

'Mrs Frampton's coming,' hissed Martin, but nobody heard him.

'You know, Tessa, if I was a size sixteen and bigger, I'd just want to die. What's it like to be so gross and disgusting, eh? You must be the ugliest girl in the whole school.'

Tessa had been trying to suppress the surge of anger that had been filling her up the way air fills a balloon. She had this sudden image of herself, fat, ugly, with woolly hair, and she just couldn't bear it, it made her feel so empty inside. With a sudden lunge, she fell on Sonia and pummelled her flat chest. 'I hate you!' she shouted. 'You rotten stinking cow!'

Sonia was gasping for breath the way that Tessa had been a moment or two earlier. She began to fight back, and kicked Tessa's shins. Then she bit deep into Tessa's arm. Tessa shrieked and punched again, but Sonia dodged aside, leaving Tessa flailing the air.

'What on earth do you think you are doing?' said Mrs Frampton. She pulled the two girls apart and glared at them coldly. 'How dare you behave like this!'

Half of Sonia's hair had slipped out of the ribbon and was hanging over her face. Her skirt was torn, and her blouse was smeared with dust. Her lip was bleeding from a small cut at the corner of her mouth. Tessa looked as bad. Her nose was starting to swell and as she pulled up the sleeve of her coat, she saw that her arm was bruised where Sonia had sunk her teeth in.

'Inside, both of you. I'm sending you to the Head.'

Sonia flushed, while Tessa looked scared. They were bundled into the cloakroom by Mrs Frampton as Martin and Jasper looked on, not sure whether they were to be included in this row or not. Mrs Frampton glanced back at them. 'I'll deal with you two later,' she said, and disappeared inside.

'Mr Cook!'

The Deputy Head turned at the sound of Mrs Frampton's voice and came towards them.

'I've just caught these two girls fighting, Mr Cook. Will you escort them to the Head? I'm still on playground duty.'

Mr Cook looked suitably disgusted to receive news of such behaviour. 'Leave them to me, Mrs Frampton,' he said.

Tessa and Sonia followed him silently up the long staircase. Tessa realized she was puffing with exertion again, and envied Sonia's easy strides. They went up two flights, and then along a long corridor. Tessa hadn't even seen the Head's office before. She couldn't imagine what would await her.

Mr Frampton knocked on a door with the name 'Mrs Tynan' on it. He waited a second or two and then went inside. Tessa and Sonia wondered if they should remain standing or sit on one of the chairs lined up against the wall. Sonia sat. She rolled down her sock and examined

79

her bruised ankle pointedly. Tessa pushed up her sleeve again and looked at her arm.

'Mrs Tynan will see you now,' said Mr Cook, putting his head round the door. Tessa and Sonia hesitated. Neither wanted to be the first inside. 'Come on, hurry up, we're waiting,' Mr Cook said with a frown, so Tessa stepped inside, pushing the door behind her so that Sonia had to stop it to avoid being smacked in the mouth. They walked past the secretary, who was typing with one hand and holding a phone with the other, and entered Mrs Tynan's office.

'Thank you, Mr Cook,' she said, and he went outside again, leaving them alone with the Head.

It was a moment or two before Tessa could bring herself to look at Mrs Tynan. She had seen her in assembly, and sometimes on the stairs, but never for long, and never this close. She was old – at least forty-five – and she had grey hairs mixed in with the black. Her hair could have been described as woolly too, and her skin was at least as dark as Tessa's own. Tessa stood on one leg. She was ashamed. She had always liked and admired Mrs Tynan, and now she had been sent to her for bad behaviour. It was all Sonia's fault. Sonia was a stinking pig.

'I understand that you two girls have been fighting.' She paused here, and Tessa wondered whether she should answer or not. The moment passed though, and Mrs Tynan went on: 'Which one of you started it?'

'She did,' they chorused, and then fell silent.

'What were you fighting about?'

Neither answered.

'It must have been about something.'

'She called me names,' said Tessa.

'What sort of names?' said Mrs Tynan, looking at Sonia.

'She just leapt on me and started punching me,' said Sonia.

'Were you calling her names?'

'Not really.'

'What do you mean, not really, Sonia? Either you were or you weren't.'

'I didn't call her anything much. Anyway, she called me things too.'

'I still want to know how this started. Tessa?'

'I was running, and she thought I looked stupid, so she called me something. Fatty, something like that, I don't remember exactly. She's always calling me things.'

'Is this true, Sonia?'

Sonia looked at the floor. 'She called me stupid. And a cow. She called me a cow.'

'Only after you called me fat guts and woolly hair!'

'All right, that's enough. It seems to me that you're both as bad as each other.'

Sonia and Tessa drew sharp breaths at the apparent injustice of this.

'First of all, I will not have name-calling in this school. It's ill-mannered and cruel, and if I hear of any more of it, you will be punished very severely indeed.' Mrs Tynan paused, and looked at each of them in turn in a very penetrating sort of way. They both looked away, and stared at the floor.

'This is a happy school —' Mrs Tynan began.

Tessa cut in suddenly, before she could stop herself. 'It's not happy. It's extremely miserable. I liked juniors much better . . .' Tessa broke off, realizing what she'd just said.

'Tessa, happiness doesn't just come to you, you have to work at it.'

Tessa scowled. This was just like her mother's dieting speech — 'Nothing don't come for nothing' and all that.

'What about you, Sonia? What do you think about the school?'

'I like it,' she answered. 'I'm very happy here.'

Mrs Tynan looked amused. 'I'm not sure I believe that either. But look, both of you, I am not going to put up with fighting. You will each do a week's detention.'

'Oh, please,' said Sonia.

Mrs Tynan merely held up her hand to indicate that there was no point in arguing. 'And during your detentions, I want each of you to write me an essay on why intolerance — whether it's on the grounds of size or shape or colour or intellect — is wrong. And I expect thoughtful, careful work from you. If I get anything less, there will be letters home to your parents. If this wasn't your first term at a new school, those letters would be going home anyway, so think yourselves lucky. And if you ever, ever fight in this school again, you will run the risk of suspension. Is that understood?'

'Yes, Mrs Tynan,' said Tessa and Sonia together.

'You may go, then, Sonia. Tessa, I'd like a word.'

Tessa remained standing by Mrs Tynan's desk, wondering why she'd been singled out for extra punishment like this.

'Sit down for a minute, dear.'

Tessa sat, bewildered at the change in Mrs Tynan's voice. She sounded almost kind.

'You say you're not happy here.'

'I didn't mean –'

'I think you did mean it, and it was an honest response. What's it about, Tessa? Can you tell me why you dislike it so much?'

Tessa thought for a moment. 'Not really.'

'Try.'

'I haven't made many friends. No girls.'

'It takes time. You have to get to know people first. You've only been here for a term, not even that.'

'I feel lost even going round the school.'

'It is a big place. I think most people feel like that when they start here, but again, it takes time. Soon, you'll wonder how you ever got lost. You don't believe me.'

Tessa smiled sheepishly. 'Not really.'

'Well, you'll just have to trust me on this. You said there have been comments about your hair. Has anyone said anything else?'

'Like what?'

'Racist remarks.'

'No, not really. Some of them think it, but they don't say it. That's why I like Jasper, he understands about it. And Martin, only . . .'

'Only what?'

83

'Martin thinks that when people say things about hair and that, they don't mean him, they only mean Jasper and me, but his parents are from Jamaica too.'

'Sometimes it's easier to pretend things like that aren't being said.'

'I suppose so,' said Tessa. 'I like Kamala too, and Trish and some others, but we're not really friends.'

'Why's that, do you think?'

'I don't know,' said Tessa, though she felt it was because she was fat.

'Tessa, you have to give new things a chance. They take time to work out. Everyone feels out of place for a while at a new school, it's not easy to settle down. You'd be surprised how many parents of new children come to me and say their son or daughter is lonely and hasn't made friends or can't find their way around the school or is frightened of the teachers. You're not alone. And it will get better. Besides, you said you do have a friend, or someone you like.'

'Jasper.'

'Well, there you are then. Some of the children in your year have nobody, and it's much harder for them.'

Tessa looked sceptical.

'You can waste a lot of time feeling sorry for yourself. You've got a lot going for you. You're bright, outgoing and articulate. Make the most of it. All right, off you go. And remember, fighting doesn't solve anything.'

It relieves your feelings though, Tessa thought, as she went through the door. Mrs Tynan had been surprisingly nice. It wasn't true about every new kid feeling out of place, though, she'd got that wrong. Most of them had settled down straight away. And it wasn't a happy school, it was miserable as sin. Tessa nursed her arm. Her nose hadn't bled, she hadn't given Sonia that satisfaction. And at least it was nearly Christmas. Two and a half weeks off school. Tessa couldn't wait.

9

The bell rang. Tessa thudded down the stairs and opened it. She grabbed her father by the hand and pulled him inside.

'Happy Christmas, darling,' he said.

'You should see the tree,' said Tessa. 'Mum and I spent all day on it, it's the best ever, you won't believe it. We chose the biggest bushiest one, and all the presents are under it, and Mum's making chocolate cake, and she's bought all the other food, except what Hetty's bringing.'

'Slow down, Tess.'

She still had him by the hand. 'Come and say hello to Mum, she's in the kitchen.'

Her father hesitated and Tessa frowned. Why couldn't he behave normally with Mum any more? It was stupid. 'Dad's here,' Tessa shouted towards the kitchen. Joy came out. 'Hello, Paul.' For a minute, it looked as though they were going to kiss each other, but then the phone rang.

'I'll get it,' said Tessa, disappointed by the interruption, but her mother was there first. 'Hi, Jan,' she said. 'It's Aunty Jan,' she announced, as if they hadn't heard. 'How are Camilla and Charmaine? I bet they're excited.'

Tessa pulled her father into the sitting-room. She didn't care whether the vile cousins were excited or not.

'Look!' she said, pointing to the tree. 'The lights from last year still work and everything. They came on straight away, the moment we plugged them in. You said you'd come early to help us decorate.'

'I got delayed on the wards. People don't stop getting sick just because it's Christmas.'

'I know that.'

'I got you something I know you're going to like.'

'What?'

'You have to wait until tomorrow, same as always.'

'Oh, Dad!'

'What's on TV? There's usually something good on Christmas Eve.'

'You don't want to watch anything, it's all boring. I thought we could do something.'

'Like what?'

'Dungeons and Dragons on the computer.'

'No, darling, I'm tired, I want to relax. We've got three days for computer games, let's have a quiet evening. I haven't had a moment to watch TV all week.'

'Dad!'

'Come on, give me a break. It's my holiday too, you know. Come and watch TV with me. Or maybe your mother needs a hand with her cake.'

'You could help her if you like.'

'I can't make a cake.'

'Neither can Mum.'

They both laughed. Paul switched on the television. There was a film on. Tessa couldn't remember what it was called, but she knew she'd seen it before, lots of times. 'Can't we watch the other side?'

'I like this,' said Paul.

'But it's already started.'

'Only ten minutes, not even that. Quiet, Tess, I'm trying to hear.'

Tessa flumped down noisily on the sofa. She picked up the *Radio Times*. 'It says here that *Trading Places* is on ITV.'

'I've seen it.'

'Well, I've seen this.'

'Tessa, stop whingeing. I want a good, peaceful Christmas, all right? You know what's wrong with you? You're too excited.'

'I am not.'

'You seem like it to me. Let's have some peace.'

'I'm going up to my room. You can have peace then, can't you?'

Tessa stomped upstairs. She wished she hadn't done that; it was childish, leaving him there. Besides, she wanted to be with him, and it was a lot more interesting than being alone in her room.

'Tessa!'

'What is it, Mum?'

'Jasper's here.'

'*Here?*'

'That's what I said. I'm sending him up.'

Jasper knocked gently on the door. Tessa opened it. 'Just come in, you don't have to knock. What's happening?'

'Nothing much. How about you?'

'I just had an argument with Dad. Good start to the festive season and all that stuff.'

'People do argue at Christmas. It's because they're all stuck in together right through the holiday trying to be happy.'

'I know what you're going to be when you grow up.'

'What?'

'A social worker.'

'No, I'm not.'

'What are you going to be then?'

'I don't know yet. Maybe a doctor like your dad. But there are things I want to do first.'

'What things?'

'It's a secret.'

Tessa looked scornful. 'Only little kids have secrets.'

'I'll tell you some time, just not now. I've brought you something.' He handed Tessa a small package.

'Your present's under the tree. I'll get it, and then we can open them together.'

'Shouldn't we save them till tomorrow?'

'Let's open them now. We'll have loads tomorrow, and there's nothing today. It'll make it more special.'

Jasper was swayed by this argument. He sat on Tessa's bed and waited for her to bring his present. He had hoped she'd get him something, but he hadn't counted on it; you just never knew with Tessa. The idea that she had thought enough of him to buy him something filled him with happiness.

'Sorry to be so long,' said Tessa. 'Hetty's just turned

up with Jonathan. Here's your present. Don't get too excited, I didn't really know what to get you.'

They were silent for a few moments with the pleasure of examining their parcels. Tessa got to her gift first. 'Brilliant,' she said, and Jasper could tell she was genuinely pleased. It had taken a lot of thought to hit on something she really wanted. She'd been saying for ages that she needed some earrings, and Jasper had paid careful attention when she'd looked at them in the shopping centre and had remembered which she'd liked. 'I can't put them on now, or Mum will know I've opened your present early, but I'll wear them tomorrow. Thanks, Jas.'

It was the first time Tessa had used this affectionate shortening of his name and Jasper liked it a lot. 'That's not the only present,' he said. 'There's something else.'

Jasper handed her a second lumpy-looking package. Tessa ripped the paper off.

'I made it,' said Jasper.

Tessa nodded. She could see that. It was an exercise book with MISFITS CLUB written in huge red letters across the cover. Inside, there was a list of rules, all the things they'd decided on in the park, like being nice to each other, and having to eat half a pound of chocolate a day. Jasper had illustrated it too, and it was like cartoons. Tessa giggled. Some of it was very funny. He was clever, Jasper was.

'There's a badge too, it must have got lost in the wrapping.'

Tessa examined the discarded paper and found a cardboard badge with a safety pin in it. 'It's really good, Jasper, thanks.'

'Put the badge on.'

Tessa pinned it to her jumper.

'I've got one too.'

Jasper took it out of his pocket. It was the same as the one he'd made for Tessa and also had caricatures of each of them on it. Tessa noted that he'd been careful not to make her look too grossly fat. She was grateful for that much. 'Well, go on, Jasper, finish opening my present. You stopped half-way through.'

Jasper unwrapped a pencil case.

'I knew you hadn't got one any more.'

'It's excellent,' said Jasper, almost speechless with pleasure. 'Thanks.'

'That's all right,' said Tessa, fingering her badge. 'Do you want to come downstairs for some Coke and mince pies? Mum's warming them up.'

'No, I have to get home, Mum said not to be long. I'll see you, Tess.'

'See you, Jasper. And thanks.' Once he'd gone, Tessa flipped through the book he'd made her again. It was kind of embarrassing. Only little kids had clubs. She took off the badge and buried it with the book in the bottom of her wardrobe. Then she sat on her bed again, but she couldn't sit still, there was so much to think about.

Tessa always buzzed with anticipation on Christmas Eve. It had begun when she was two or three years old and had first heard about Father Christmas. She'd lain awake at night in the hope of catching him leaving a stocking in her room. She'd never managed it, of course, and at six she'd discovered he was just a fairy tale, but the excitement and the hope remained. She wished she hadn't clouded it with that argument with her father. She went back into the living-room. He was still watching TV, a different programme now. There was some woman on the screen lounging about in a bikini. Such programmes irritated Tessa. Nobody was that good-looking in real life – or at least she hoped they weren't. 'Can't we watch something else, Dad? It's my turn to choose now.' Tessa knew she was whingeing again, but she couldn't help herself.

'I'm in the middle of it. You were upstairs with Jasper.'

'It looks like a load of rubbish anyway. That woman's awful.'

'Good-looking though,' said her father, his mind clearly on the programme.

'She's too thin,' said Tessa, hoping that he would agree, but he said nothing, he just carried on watching. 'Do you really like her?'

'What, darling?'

'That woman. Do you really like her?'

'It's just TV, Tessa,' he said, but he continued to give it all his attention. Tessa looked down at her knees. They bulged out in front of her in just the way Sonia had described them on the day of the fight. Maybe if she'd looked more like the woman on the TV screen, her dad wouldn't have gone to live somewhere else, and would be home all the time, not just for visits on Christmas and Easter. And maybe she'd have more friends, and maybe things would be easier, happier, more fun. Maybe she wouldn't need to belong to a Misfits Club with Jasper.

Tessa went into the kitchen. 'Hi, Mum, how's the chocolate cake?'

'Want some?'

Tessa shook her head.

'Doctor, come quick, save my daughter from death.' Joy felt Tessa's forehead with mock concern.

'I'm all right, Mum, honest.' Tessa sat at the table. 'Where's Hetty?'

'Gone next door with Jonathan to wish Mrs Meadows a happy Christmas.'

'Can you only get thin by going on a diet?'

'It's the only way I know. And exercise, but diet is the most important thing. But wait until after Christmas, love. You'll never manage it over the holiday, it's more than flesh and blood could deal with.'

Tessa nodded. After Christmas then. She tried to imagine life without chocolate, ice cream and chips, but it was beyond her. It would be dull, that was for sure, and miserable, too. The only question was, would it be more miserable than being fat? It was hard to decide.

10

'Tessa, your dad wants to speak to you,' called Joy.

Tessa gave a squeal of relief and excitement. He hadn't called her since Christmas, and he usually rang at least once a week. She'd been afraid that she'd done something to upset him.

She hadn't enjoyed Christmas this year at all. It was the first one that hadn't been what she'd anticipated. Every now and then, the disappointment of it flooded over her. She'd hoped that the season of good will would have made her parents kinder to each other, but if anything, it had been the opposite. There had been no actual rows while she was around, but she'd felt the undercurrents all right. Hope that her mum and dad would realize how much better everything would be if they got back together again was fading fast.

Tessa picked up the receiver eagerly. 'Hiya, Dad.'

'Hello, darling. How are you doing?'

'OK.'

'How's school?'

'All right. Same as usual.'

'Your mother says you've been happier there lately.'

'I'm getting more used to it.'

'How's your boyfriend?'

Tessa sat down heavily on the floor beside the phone. 'Dad! He's not my boyfriend. He's just someone I talk to.'

Her father chuckled at the other end of the line. It was just one of his usual wind-ups, but she fell for them every time. 'I've got some news, Tess.'

Tessa stiffened. He was preparing her for something bad, she could tell by the tone of his voice. 'What news?' she said.

'I've got another job.'

She relaxed a little. Was that all? 'That's good,' she said, feeling that this was expected of her.

'Tessa darling, it means a move.'

'A move? Where to?'

'It's a hospital near Brighton.'

'Brighton? But that's miles away. When will I see you? You can't move there, it's stupid, it's too far.'

'It's a good post, it involves research. It's something I've been hoping to get into for a long time.'

'But what about me? And Mum?'

'I'll still see you most weekends. Brighton's only an hour from Victoria Station.'

'But I can't just come round after school if I want to talk to you, can I?'

'How often do you do that, Tess?'

Tessa felt anger and frustration rising inside her. He was refusing to understand how bad this was going to be. 'That's not the point. The point is, I could if I wanted to. Now I can't.'

'I'll still be there for you, Tessa. You only have to pick up a phone, you know that.'

'Why do you have to go? I don't see why you left in the first place. What good has it done? Don't you care any more?'

'Tessa, how can you ask that?'

The answer was obvious. He'd gone away. And she was left with her mother, missing him. Her mother kept on dieting because she thought it would make people like her more, especially Dad. Maybe that was why he'd gone, because she, Tessa, was so fat and ugly that nobody in their right mind would want to be in the same house with her. He was sick of her being such a great fat ugly lump. Her greed had forced him away from her.

'Tessa, speak to me, darling.'

'No!' she shouted, and slammed down the phone. She picked it up again immediately, but it was too late, there was just a buzz. She continued to sit there for a moment or two, hoping that he would call her back, but nothing happened. She wondered if she should ring him, but he would probably be angry with her and she couldn't deal with that, not now. She trudged back up the stairs and went into her bedroom. She wanted to slam the door, but she didn't dare in case her mother heard and came up to see what was wrong, She wanted to be alone for a while, to think.

She lay on top of her new duvet. She'd just persuaded her mother that the Barbie Doll print she'd had since she was five was too young for her now, and she'd helped to choose a really grown-up one in cream with broderie anglaise frills. It made the whole room seem lighter. She had a couple of posters on the walls, from her favourite films, but they were out of date already and she wanted to get some new ones. She didn't know what other girls her age liked because she didn't really know any. Didn't really want to. They just made her look even more hefty and clumsy than she already was, and she envied them so painfully that it was best just to be alone, or with Jasper. At least he made her feel like she was worth something. She began to cry. She was angry with her dad, and sad that she mattered so little that he could go away from her. The idea that he was leaving made her stomach cramp. She reached under her pillow for her secret supply of M & Ms and popped a large handful into her mouth. It was stupid, the more fed up with herself she felt, the more she ate, and so it went on, a vicious circle that she couldn't break.

'Tessa.' Joy's voice came through the door.

'What is it, Mum?'

Joy opened the door and came in, uninvited. Tessa pushed the M & Ms packet back under the pillow, hoping she'd been quick enough to hide them. 'I knew your father's news would upset you,' said Joy.

'I'm not upset,' Tessa lied.

'It's not that far, Brighton. And I know how much he wanted that job. He's waited far too long for promotion – he needs this.'

'Why are you being so understanding about it? You don't usually take his side.'

Joy sighed. 'There shouldn't be sides.'

'But there are, you know there are.'

'Not any more. It's not fair on anyone. If your dad goes to Brighton, it won't affect how he feels about you, really it won't. He's always adored you.'

'He likes Hetty best.'

'That's not true.'

'Hetty's pretty.'

'Well, so are you.'

'I'm fat.'

'Since when has that bothered you?'

'Since forever,' said Tessa, allowing the tears to drip from her cheeks.

'Come on, Tess. You'll see more of your dad because he'll have whole weekends free. He won't be on call any more, this is a research job.'

'What does that mean?'

'It means he won't be dealing with patients like he does now, or not so much. He'll have more time.'

Tessa rubbed her eyes with the long scrap of toilet paper she kept for wiping chocolate from her fingers. 'If he's in Brighton, it doesn't matter if he has more time or not.'

'You're determined to see this as some sort of tragedy, love, and it isn't. It won't change anything for you, you'll see your dad as often as ever. And it's by the sea. Think what fun you could have in summer.'

Tessa pictured herself having fun in a little bikini. She was horrified at the thought. 'I don't like the sea. It's boring.'

'Well, if you're determined to feel sorry for yourself, there's nothing I can do to stop you,' said Joy, getting to her feet.

'No, there isn't, so don't bother trying, OK?'

'Tessa –'

'It means he isn't coming back here to live, doesn't it? It must do.'

'Tessa, I don't know, love, but I don't think –'

'That's the phone ringing. I'll get it!'

Tessa ran down the stairs again and picked up the phone nervously. But it wasn't her father's voice she heard.

'Is that Tessa Hislop? It's Jasper Woodrow here.'

'Jasper, what are you doing phoning me?'

There was a long silence. Then he said, 'I just felt like it. Are you OK, Tess? You sound funny, sort of muffled.'

Tessa realized she wasn't managing to disguise the sound of her crying as effectively as she'd imagined. 'I'm all right,' she said.

'What's the matter?'

Tessa sat on the carpet again. She hadn't thought of Jasper as someone to tell her worst troubles to, but he was there, and he was kind, and he cared what happened to her. 'My dad's moving to Brighton.'

'Are you scared you won't see him any more?'

'Yes,' Tessa whispered.

'You will. He'll make certain.'

'How do you know?'

'Because I saw you and him together that time I stayed. He really cares about you, Tess, he'd never just go away.'

'You really do believe that? You're absolutely sure?'

'Absolutely,' said Jasper, with such certainty that Tessa was almost convinced.

'I have to go now, in case my dad rings again. Thanks for phoning me. I'll see you tomorrow, Jasper.'

'See you tomorrow, Tess.'

Joy came down the stairs. 'Was that your dad?'

'No, it was Jasper.'

'What did he want?'

Tessa thought about it. She really wasn't sure. 'Just to chat, I think. He's all right, Jasper is.'

'Well, he seems to have cheered you up, anyhow. Shall I make you some hot chocolate? I've got some of that low-calorie stuff. It's nice.'

Tessa nodded, though she preferred thick Cadbury's, not the dish-water substitute. Still, she wanted something sweet and warming, and it was chocolate, after a fashion.

Joy was obviously expecting a mother and daughter session. They each clutched a mug and sipped the bland liquid, trying to feel closer to one another and getting nowhere. After a few minutes, Tessa pretended to be tired and said she was going to bed.

The radio alarm clock in her room showed half past nine. Tessa sprawled across the bed and wished she felt like reading. Jasper would have written his English essay by now but she hadn't even thought about it. Still, what was homework compared to major family trauma? What did it matter whether it was done or not? Tessa began to undress slowly, trying not to see her enormous stomach and jubbly legs. It wasn't fair that she looked so ugly, it just wasn't. Across the room, set in a long row, was a shelf of the dolls she had been collecting since she was a sprog. They stared back at her, mockingly. Sindys and Barbies, not just one of each, but lots of different varieties, some with dark hair, some blonde. Tessa liked the blonde ones best. They were the proper ones. Blue-eyed and pale-skinned, they showed Tessa exactly what she wasn't. Sometimes she resented them for it, but mostly she felt a wistful kind of envy. If only she had such long, slim legs, and neat little feet and long hair. The hair was a particularly sore point. The Afro-Caribbean hair Tessa possessed would never grow long like that, and it didn't hang down neatly, it frizzed out all over the place. When she was really little, Tessa had been given an old Barbie-type doll called Tressie. It had been her mother's, and it had a button in the middle of its stomach and if you pushed it and tugged its hair, it grew out of the top of its head until it was waist-length. Then you could put a key in and turn it, and as you did, the hair went short again. Tessa would have given anything to have hair like that. She had wanted it for as long as she could remember. You couldn't be glamorous and nice-looking with hair like hers, you needed the sort of hair that dolls had to be any good at all. Yet as she thought about it, Tessa felt guilty for wishing she had different hair because she knew she ought to be proud of what she was, and of being black. But Sindy and Barbie were perfect, and Sindy and Barbie were mostly white, or dark-skinned with long hair and pointed noses, not flat noses like the one Tessa had.

Sonia looked like a Barbie. She was pretty and slim, and she had a girlie walk. Tessa envied her, how she envied her! Just thinking about how much she wanted to be Sonia kept her awake at night.

Joy came barging in again. Tessa pulled her duvet round her, trying to hide her wobbling shape. She wished her mother would learn to knock. It wasn't fair to come straight in like that, it showed a lack of sensitivity.

'Aren't you in bed yet?' asked Joy in surprise. 'I thought you were tired. It's nearly half past ten, and you know how bad you are in the mornings.'

'I'm trying to get undressed. I'd have been ready by now if you hadn't come and interrupted me.'

'Less of your cheek, Tess. Come on, give me a goodnight kiss.'

Tessa moved her lips towards her mother and tried to kiss her without actually touching her. It wasn't that she didn't want to, it was more that she felt so shy and stupid and awkward, she just couldn't seem to bring herself to do it. Her mother seemed satisfied, though.

'Goodnight, love, see you tomorrow. And don't worry about your dad, he won't be all that far away, really he won't. It's only an hour on the train.'

'Goodnight, Mum,' said Tessa grumpily. 'Switch the light off as you go.'

The darkness was reassuring. Tessa couldn't see herself. She felt protected and safe when the lights were out. She wished there wasn't any daylight and it could be dark all the time, and no one ever had to look at anybody else. That would be heaven, she thought.

11

'Tessa, it's quarter past eight!'

Tessa fought with herself. What had her mother just said? She didn't want to hear it, she only wanted to sleep. The radio was playing her favourite song. She listened drowsily to the words; it was about two young people nobody liked who'd found each other. Her and Jasper. As the thought struck her, it filled her with uneasiness. She didn't want to have to depend on someone like Jasper for anything. And besides, she certainly wasn't in love with him, it was mad even to think it. He was too short, for one thing, and his glasses were too thick.

And you're too fat, said a voice inside her head.

But I could be beautiful, Tessa answered herself. I'm not really ugly, I'm not always going to be like this.

'Tessa!'

She jumped as her mother's voice reached her. What time was it? She looked at the digits on the face of the radio. 8.25, it said. 'Oh hell and damn!' said Tessa, half-throwing herself out of bed and running to the bathroom.

By the time she came downstairs, her mother had already gone. No chance of a lift, then. 'It isn't fair,' Tessa muttered. 'It just isn't fair.' If she hadn't stayed awake half the night worrying about Brighton, she wouldn't have overslept. Now she'd be late, and it was all her dad's fault. She hated him.

Jasper's prim voice cut into her thoughts. *It's wrong to hate people*. But it was so satisfying. And so much less boring than loving everyone all the time.

Tessa picked up her bag and ran through the door, only just remembering to check that she'd shut it properly. She hadn't, so she slammed it again, sighing with relief. If she'd let burglars in, her mother would have pulverized her, and it was bad enough to have one parent treating her badly, she didn't want two. She began to do a slow jog, but she was winded before she'd even reached the corner, and the sweat was trickling round her ears and leaving damp patches under her arms. They'd done sweat in biology, along with the heart and the liver and all kinds of other sick-making things. If only she didn't have a body. If only no one did. Then she wouldn't have to think about how stupid she looked all the time. And maybe someone other than Jasper would start liking her.

It was ten past nine before she got to the school gate. The street was so still, it reminded her of a town in a Western when the baddies had just stormed in on horseback and frightened everyone indoors. It was eerie, the aloneness of it. She'd only ever been near school when it was bustling with boys and girls charging about all over the place.

She walked slowly across the playground. There was no point in hurrying any more, she was too late for it to matter. The rest of the class would be in first lesson now

– English, or French. She walked upstairs, pausing to get her breath, and peered through the pane of glass that filled the upper portion of her classroom door. Sonia's head shot up, but Tessa had good reflexes. She ducked down too fast to be seen. For a moment, Tessa considered just walking out of school again, and having the day off. Who would know? She could find some way of covering her tracks, she was clever enough. But supposing they told her mother, or even her dad? Tessa had been late when she was in the juniors. No one took much notice. But here, it was different. It was illegal to use the cane any more, she'd heard Sonia saying that, but teachers weren't stupid, and if they weren't allowed to hit you nowadays, they'd probably thought up something even more awful to take its place. Tessa's imagination failed to supply a horrible enough alternative, but she had no doubt there was one. It was that sort of school. Her best bet was to go to the classroom where they'd be for the second lesson and to wait outside until the others came.

The bell rang sooner than Tessa had expected. It made her jump. She flattened herself against the wall as dozens of fifth formers swarmed round her. Some of the boys were six feet tall. Their voices had broken. And the girls wore high heels, in defiance of the rules. One girl even wore red ones, quite fearlessly. Tessa admired the daring of such an act, and tried to imagine how she would look when she was fifteen and in the fifth form. She'd have long hair, for a start. And dainty thin legs which she'd set off with strappy shoes, like the ones her sister had worn at her wedding. They'd be gold lamé, or snakeskin, and Sonia would want to know where she'd got them from.

By the fifth form, Sonia would be well into decline. Her hair would be bleached coarse and dull, and she would have developed a chest so enormous that she would look as if she were about to fall on her face whenever she walked from the sheer weight of it. Her legs would bulge over knee-socks, the kind that elderly ladies wore instead of tights, and the wind would lift her skirt every now and then to reveal the horrible way their elastic was cutting into Sonia's ample flesh. Her upper arms would wobble and she'd have such acne that she would have been quarantined twice with suspected bubonic plague. As Tessa contemplated this, with a smile on her face, Sonia bounced towards her, sickeningly full of health. 'I told Mr Davis you weren't at the lesson in case he didn't notice. I didn't want you to miss out on French translation homework.'

'Thanks,' said Tessa, in a voice that was heavy with sarcasm. What a grass Sonia was. Why didn't anyone except Jasper ever seem to notice? You can't fool all of the people all of the time, that's what Tessa's mother said. But Sonia seemed to manage it.

'Where were you?' said Jasper, joining Tessa in the line outside the Geography room.

Sonia moved on to talk to Martin, so Tessa said, 'I overslept.'

'You didn't miss much. French was boring as usual. Sonia grassed you up. Old Davis wouldn't have noticed you weren't there if she hadn't helped him to it.'

106

Tessa shrugged. There wasn't anything she could do about that now. She would rather not think about the trouble she was in.

'At the end of the lesson, I asked Mr Davis what happened if people were late. He said nothing much, just a detention, only twenty minutes and nothing very hard to do in it.'

Tessa knew how shy Jasper was and how much it would have taken for him to go up to a teacher and find out something like that. And he'd done it for her. 'Thanks,' she said, in her warmest voice. Jasper smiled as they filed into class.

Nothing much happened in Geography either. Jasper got a good mark for his homework, and Tessa wasn't far behind. Miss Poole said well done to both of them. At the end of the lesson, Tessa asked Jasper what was next. He looked surprised that she didn't already know. 'Games,' he answered, after a little pause.

Tessa went numb at the thought. 'I haven't got my kit,' she said in a quivering voice.

'It will be all right,' said Jasper with a confidence he was only pretending to feel.

'Remember that time at register when Mrs Frampton said Miss Jenkins would make me do it in my vest and knickers if I forgot again?'

'She was bluffing.'

'What if she wasn't? I'm going home.' Tessa picked up her bag and coat and began to run along the corridor, dodging the thirty fourth formers who were moving to an art lesson in the opposite direction.

'Tessa Hislop, where do you think you are going?'

Tessa stopped dead. She tried to think of a means of escape but there was none. She was trapped.

Miss Jenkins looked her up and down, seeming to take pleasure in her discomfort. 'I said, where do you think you are going?'

'Nowhere, Miss Jenkins.'

'I hope you're going along to the changing-room. You need the fresh air, not to mention the exercise. Come along, we mustn't waste any more time if we're going to get you into shape.'

Those within hearing laughed, and Tessa hung her head. Why, oh why had she forgotten to pick up her kit that morning? She'd give anything to have remembered it. Slow death by ants eating you in the sands of the desert had got to be better than this.

Jasper went off with Sir who did boys' games. Tessa trailed after Miss Jenkins, who turned around every now and then to check that she was still there. They arrived outside the girls' changing-room, which Miss Jenkins unlocked. They each stood in front of a peg and everyone but Tessa began to strip. Tessa kept her eyes on the floor.

'Don't dawdle, Tessa Hislop. Where's your kit?'

Tessa didn't answer.

'Don't tell me you've forgotten it again? I simply don't believe it.'

Kamala, who was a thin but sensitive girl, looked anxiously at Tessa, as if she were hoping that it wasn't true. The others giggled, hoping that it was.

108

'Well, I have warned you, Tessa.'

'I can't do it.'

'Can't do what?'

'Games in my knickers,' Tessa whispered.

'She'll be doing something else in her knickers in a minute,' Sonia said.

'Be quiet!' snapped Miss Jenkins.

'Please,' said Tessa.

'How many times have I told you what would happen if you persisted in coming without your top and shorts?'

There was a significant pause, which Tessa finally filled with a soft, 'I don't know.'

'Too many times, Tessa Hislop. Far too many times. You'd better get undressed.'

'I can't.'

'You should have thought of the consequences of forgetfulness, shouldn't you? All right, Tessa, this is your last warning, and I mean it. No, don't sit down. I still expect to see you out there on that netball court.'

'But —'

'Go and look in lost property. Find a kit there to put on. I've got an old pair of plimsolls that are about your size. You can wear those too. Then perhaps you'll remember for next time.'

'Stinking bully,' muttered Tessa under her breath as Miss Jenkins turned away from her to find the shoes.

Still with her back turned, Miss Jenkins said, 'Well, go on, Tessa, start looking for another kit. You've got three minutes.'

Tessa hurried into the small back room where the bats

109

and balls and hockey sticks were kept. There was a box labelled lost property. She delved into it and pulled out several grubby shirts and two pairs of shorts. She held them up. They wouldn't fit, of course they wouldn't.

'Bring them out here, Tessa.'

Tessa emerged slowly.

'Show them to me.'

Miss Jenkins examined them carefully. 'There, this should fit, and this. Get changed. Hurry up.'

Kamala cast her sympathetic looks, but everyone else stared as she began to pull off her jumper. In a minute, they'd see her bra and they'd laugh themselves hoarse. Tessa stopped undressing.

'What are you waiting for, Tessa? Come on, the rest of you should be ready by now. Outside. Quickly.'

Tessa went limp with relief as the other girls left the changing-room, their sighs showing that their fun had been spoilt.

'I'll see you outside in one minute, Tessa,' Miss Jenkins said.

It took Tessa more than a minute to get into the gym shirt, and to force herself into the shorts. The shirt was pulled so tightly over her front that she looked like an overstuffed cushion. The side zip on the shorts wouldn't do up, and the legs cut into her thighs so that she could hardly walk for fear of splitting the material.

Miss Jenkins came back in again. 'Out you come, Tessa,' she said, and she led her into the playground.

Everybody stopped to watch. Tessa limped on to the concrete, not looking at anyone. Over on the far side, the boys turned too, and gazed across at her, sniggering and making dirty remarks. Jasper's face was set in an angry, hurt expression, as if he were the one to suffer the humiliation, not Tess. One of the girls threw the heavy netball towards her. Tessa instinctively reached for it, and as she caught it clumsily in her arms, the seam of her shirt tore with a loud rending sound.

'All right, everyone, get on with the game. Tessa, you can go inside now. It's obvious that you won't be much use dressed like that. Off you go and get changed. And remember that the price for persistent forgetfulness is high.'

Tessa sloped indoors. She changed back into her school skirt and jumper as quickly as she could. She refused to cry; she wouldn't give them the satisfaction. But she locked herself in the toilets until it was time for break.

12

Tessa avoided everyone for the rest of the day. She slipped into each lesson at the last minute and was the first to leave. At dinner time she went out for some chips, and ate two burgers and a box of chicken nuggets. If she was fat, she might as well get fatter. What difference did it make?

She gave Jasper the slip at home time and got on a bus to the shops. She wandered round the glitzy shopping centre, pausing to watch the water splashing round the fountain. People had thrown coins; you could make a wish. Tessa threw a fifty pence piece into the middle of the water and wished with all her heart that she were thin.

She went to Miss Selfridge and looked in through the glass. This season's colours were orange and lime. She'd look like a sick parrot in them. She turned away, wondering how anyone fitted into those little tube tops. They weren't made for real human beings, they were made for mutants.

It was comforting, thinking that she was normal, and that the rest of the world was strange. Why should it be her that was wrong and out of step all the time? What was so wonderful about being a size ten anyway? Did it make you happy?

Yes.

That was the trouble. Tessa could believe all too easily that being a size ten would make her very, very happy. The happiest girl in the world.

She went into Smiths. On the top shelf, there were magazines that told fat people how to get slim. Tessa took one down very carefully, and opened it as if she were reading something rude. She didn't want to be seen looking at it. Everyone would laugh at her for being stupid enough to think she could ever look different. Also, she didn't want anyone to know how much she minded about being fat, and if she were seen reading one of those magazines people would think she cared.

The pages were full of fatties, but these were the Before pictures. There were After pictures too, of the fatties once they'd got thin. Some of them had lost five or six stone. One woman had lost ten stone and was less than half the weight she'd been before. Tessa held out her arm and tried to imagine it without so much flesh on it. Her imagination failed her. It wouldn't work. Once you were fat, that was it, you were stuck with it. She replaced the magazine and left the shop, but once she was outside, she wished she'd had the bottle to buy it. She sneaked back inside and bought two different slimming magazines that she knew she would only read in darkest secrecy. She couldn't wait until she got them home though, so she hid them in the folds of her raincoat and smuggled them into the ladies' toilet, locking the cubicle door behind her.

They made fascinating reading. Yes, You Can Be Slim, one article said. It explained about calories and how you got fat when you ate more than your body was able to convert into energy. The only answer was diet and exercise, the more exercise, the better. Tessa groaned.

Someone banged on the door.

'Are you all right, dear?'

'Yes,' answered Tessa, hoping that her voice covered her embarrassment.

'Only you sound as if you might be ill, and you've been in there an awful long time.'

'No, I'm all right, really.' Tessa closed her eyes and listened, hoping that the woman would go away. At last, she heard the footsteps fading. She opened the door and slipped out.

On the bus home, Tessa thought about calories. How many did she eat in a day? How much did chips, Mars bars, toffees, milkshakes, and the odd pork pie amount to? And that was only the between meals stuff. Oh hell, it was hopeless.

The phone was ringing as Tessa walked through the front door. It was probably Jasper. She decided not to answer it. How would he understand what it had felt like to be laughed at in that stupid games kit? It wasn't the same for boys; if you were a boy, no one expected you to look wonderful all the time. You could be clever and it didn't seem odd. If you were a girl, and you were clever and ugly, you might as well give up, because no one would ever give you any respect, that was for sure.

The phone stopped ringing. 'Tessa, did you answer that?' her mother shouted.

'Wrong number,' Tessa lied.

Joy came out of the kitchen, rubbing the flour on her hands across the front of her apron. 'I thought I'd make a cake. You seem like you could do with cheering up at the moment.'

Tessa tried to look pleased. She wanted that cake, she could smell it, chocolate and rich, and moist to the touch. But she wanted to be thin, too.

'I'm thinking of going on a diet,' she said.

'I've made the cake now. Start tomorrow,' answered her mother.

Tessa nodded vigorously, grateful for having been given an honourable way out. 'Yes,' she said, 'tomorrow will do.'

Tessa's mother was calling her. She could tell it was late by the tone of Joy's voice. Tessa remembered the groaning that had so alarmed the woman in the toilet the previous day. She decided to try it out, and writhed once or twice for good measure.

But Tessa's mother only laughed. 'Games today, is it?'

'It was yesterday.'

'Well, if you're going to make me believe you're ill, you'll have to come up with something that sounds a little less terminal. Anyone who needed to moan like that would have been rushed to hospital in an ambulance during the night.'

'I have got a pain,' said Tessa feebly.

Her mother touched Tessa's forehead. 'Quite cool. Come on, Tess, what's the matter? Have you and Jasper fallen out?'

'No, it's got nothing to do with him.'

'What then?'

Tessa hadn't meant to tell, but the fact that her mother was willing to take the time to listen made her want to confess. 'Everyone's laughing at me because I'm so fat.'

Joy sat on the edge of the bed. 'Kids can be cruel, I know that.'

'It's true though, isn't it? I am fat. You think I am. You're always telling me to go on a diet.'

'It's not that you don't look nice as you are, lovey. It's just that you could look even nicer.'

Tessa turned her head to the wall.

'You mustn't be so sensitive about it, you know.'

Tessa pulled the bedclothes up around her head. 'I wish no one ever had to look at me,' she said.

Joy laughed. 'Come on, Tess, you're being silly. You make everything into a big drama. You could do with losing a few pounds, that's all.'

'I can't lose weight, I've tried. Anyway, why can't people like me fat?'

'People do like you.'

'No they don't. Only Jasper.'

'You're going to be late.'

'Do I have to go, Mum? They were rotten to me yesterday. Can't I stay here?'

'No, Tess. If you do, it'll be all the harder tomorrow. Honest it will. I used to get teased at school.'

'But Mum, you're thin.'

'I wasn't teased because of my size. I was the only black kid in my class, and I got teased about that.'

116

'It's not fair, is it?'

'No, it's not, Tess. But the only way to deal with it is to face it and not to run away.'

Tessa sighed. Grown-ups always said things like that, it was part of their patter, but you'd have to be out of your head to be taken in by it because they ran away themselves all the time. Tessa remembered when her mum and dad had split up, and how much running they'd both done then, not to places, but inside themselves, not talking about anything and pretending it wasn't happening. Grown-ups were such hypocrites.

'Come on, Tess, up you get, or you'll be late, and that won't help anything either.'

Tessa looked out for Jasper as she slowly made her way to school, but she didn't see him. She didn't know if she wanted to talk to him or not, but she needed to know he was there. Once she reached the playground, she expected to find him by the shed where he usually waited for her if they hadn't already managed to meet, but there was no one there. And then suddenly she saw him, jogging slowly towards her, a big soppy grin on his face.

'Hiya, Tessa. Are you OK?'

'Why shouldn't I be?'

Jasper didn't know if he should mention the games incident or not. He didn't want Tessa to be upset all over again. If she wanted to pretend it hadn't happened, maybe he should let her, he decided. So all he said was, 'No reason.' Then he added kindly, 'It's maths first lesson. You'll like that, won't you?'

Tessa wanted to tell him that she wasn't a baby and she didn't need him to be so sickly nice to her. But at the same time, his kindness was making her feel warm inside, and it seemed mean to kick him in the teeth for it. She followed him into the school as the bell went, ignoring the snide remarks of Sonia and her cronies. She didn't care anyway, she told herself, and she'd rather be fat than be cruel.

At break-time, Jasper produced a Mars bar. 'Here you are, Tess,' he said. 'I thought it would cheer you up.'

Tessa looked at it, imagining how good it would taste. But she had to be strong. 'I don't want it,' she said coldly.

Jasper looked bewildered. 'But it's your favourite,' he said.

'No,' said Tessa, a note of desperation creeping into her voice. She began to walk towards the sheds, out of temptation's way.

Jasper was following her. 'Have I done something to upset you?' he asked, barely hiding his panic.

'No, Jasper.'

'I got it specially for you,' he said.

'Jasper, TAKE IT OUT OF MY SIGHT!'

He was still following her, she could hear him. She looked over her shoulder. He was walking with his head down, seeming as if he was going to cry. Tessa stopped. 'It's not you, Jasper. I've got to go on a diet. See?' Warmth flooded Tessa's face as she made this admission. It was so embarrassing to say it, and she was ashamed of herself, the way she looked, and the fact that a diet was necessary.

'You're fine the way you are,' said Jasper.

Tessa almost smiled. He sounded as if he believed it. But how could he? She was fat, fat, fat.

'Why do you want to go on a diet?'

Jasper really seemed to want to know. Tessa could see that it was a puzzle to him. They sat down on a damp wooden bench. 'Everybody laughed at me,' Tessa said.

'They laugh at everyone. They laugh at me too.'

'Yes, but you don't mind.'

'Of course I mind,' said Jasper. 'But they're not worth it. I know they're not, and it's stopping me minding so much.'

'Sometimes, you talk just like a grown-up,' said Tessa. It wasn't meant as a compliment.

Jasper shrugged. He didn't see what Tessa meant. He felt really young all the time, and he especially felt young when he was with Tessa, because she knew so much about things. 'Don't go on a diet,' Jasper said. He didn't know why, but the thought of Tessa getting thin scared him. He could picture her getting slimmer and slimmer until she was hardly there at all, and was a sort of nothingness in front of him. 'Don't go on a diet, Tess,' he repeated.

Tessa laughed. 'You sound so serious,' she said. 'I tell you what. I'll have half the Mars bar with you. OK?'

'OK,' said Jasper, and he solemnly broke it in two. 'Tessa, I want to ask you something.'

'Well, go on then.'

'You don't have to or anything.'

'Don't have to what?'

119

'I mean, you can say no.'

'What is it, Jasper?'

'Will you come round to my house for tea next week?'

'Sure, if you like.'

'Really?'

'Of course, stupid. Why's it such a big deal?'

Jasper was starting to wonder about that himself. He'd been so sure she'd refuse that he hadn't been able to summon the courage to ask her, even though he'd been wanting to for weeks.

'Can I have a bite of your Mars bar now? I knew I wouldn't be able to stop once I'd started. That's the trouble with food. You always end up wanting more,' Tessa said.

Jasper handed it over. That was the trouble with life in general, he thought. Whenever one nice thing happened, you ended up wanting more and more until you got greedy for nice things to happen over and over. Liking Tess was like that. He seemed to want her company all the time now, and he was miserable when he couldn't spend time with her. But at least she had said yes to coming to tea with him. What if she didn't enjoy it? What if she didn't like the flat or his room or anything? He was looking forward to having her visit him there, but he was scared too.

'What's the matter now, Jasper?' said Tessa in an irritable way.

'I'm all right,' he said.

She handed him the last morsel of Mars. 'And don't ever say I don't give you anything,' she said with laughter as Jasper popped it in his mouth.

13

Tessa had been crying. Her eyes had swollen so much that she could hardly see. Why had she let herself get so fat? If she hadn't eaten those ten million chocolate bars, none of this misery would have been necessary. But then, that was the trouble with being overweight. You felt so guilty all the time. Everything you read told you, one way or another, that it was your own fault for being such a greedy slob. Fatties should have some self-control, they shouldn't be so gluttonous. That was a horrible word, gluttonous. Did it really exist, or had she made it up? It made you think of someone with fleshy bits hanging off them and huge lumps where no lumps ought to be. Gluttonous. It was the sort of word that Jasper would like.

Joy came into the kitchen and put some bread in the toaster. 'Do you want a slice?' she asked.

Tessa shook her head.

'I don't like to see you so miserable. I've been thinking, Tess. If you really want to lose weight, you should go to a slimming club. They've got one for kids, you won't even have to be with the grown-ups, and they give you some nice menus, you'll hardly know you're slimming at all because the food will be really tasty.'

Tessa thought of the awfulness of doing all this in public. Didn't they weigh you every week in front of

121

everyone at slimming clubs? She'd be the fattest kid there, easily. And the others would laugh and think secretly that no one as gross as she was could ever be thin. 'No,' she said, 'I don't want to do it.'

'I think you should, Tess. Maybe then you'll feel better about yourself, and not need to grouch so much. Why don't I ring them up this afternoon? Just give it one go. Then, if you don't like it, you needn't go back.'

'Do you promise I won't have to stay if I don't like it there?'

'I promise.'

'OK, you can phone then,' said Tessa.

The first meeting was the following Monday afternoon in a hall near the church. Tessa's mother dropped her there in the car.

'No, don't come in, Mum,' Tessa said.

'I have to come with you, love. You're not going to be cooking your own meals, are you? I have to know what sort of food they want me to do for you.'

'Please, Mum.'

'Don't be silly, Tess,' said Joy, and she took her firmly by the arm and escorted her up the hall steps.

There were four other children there already, three girls and a boy. The grown-ups sat on one side of the room, the children on the other, so Tessa joined them. The girls smiled shyly in her direction, but the boy stared straight ahead and didn't look at anyone. Tessa tried to gauge how fat the others were in relation to her. One girl was enormous, the largest kid Tessa had ever seen. She was mousy-haired and spotty and she was chewing gum. 'Do you want a bit?' she said, as she caught Tessa watching her. 'It hasn't got any calories.'

Tessa took a piece so as not to seem unfriendly. There was something comforting about being able to chew for as long as you wanted without guilt, knowing it wouldn't make you any fatter.

'What's your name?' said a girl who looked Chinese and who, in terms of size, fitted somewhere between Tessa and the mega fatty. She had a round face and a deep fringe that was cut very neatly. Her hair was tied at the sides with ribbons.

'I'm Tessa Hislop.'

'I'm Lucy Szu. I'm ten and a half. This is Julie Southey,' she said, pointing to the largest of them. 'She's nearly twelve. The one on the other side of you is Mary Nolan.'

'I'm nine,' said Mary quickly, obviously wanting the chance to speak for herself.

Lucy paused for a moment and then went on, 'The boy with the sulks is David Gerrard. He's thirteen.'

'Have you been before?' asked Tessa.

'Loads of times. I've lost nearly a stone.'

'Honest?'

Lucy nodded. 'Julie's lost a stone and a half.'

Tessa looked at Julie in disbelief. At last, she'd met someone even bigger than herself. She'd had no idea such people existed. Tessa felt excited, and superior. She wasn't the worst guzzler in the world after all.

Two more boys came into the room, and another girl.

123

Tessa wondered why the girl was there. She looked fine – normal, in fact. 'That's Gemma Newman,' whispered Lucy. 'They think she's going to get the child slimmer of the year award. They've taken photographs and everything.'

Tessa stared across at Gemma, who was coming over to join them.

'She's lost four stone,' Lesley continued. 'She's fourteen. She's really pretty, isn't she?'

Gemma was wearing leggings and a baggy sweater, the kind of clothes Tessa was itching to be seen in. It was possible, then.

A solemn-looking woman and a thin man walked into the room, and silence fell instantly. 'Hello, everyone and welcome,' said the woman. 'I'm Janice Ryder, and this is Bill Evans. I know most of you, of course, but I believe we have two new members here this afternoon. Could you stand up, please, Tessa Hislop.'

Tessa got to her feet, awkward with the embarrassment of it. She sat down again almost at once.

'And where's Danny Lever?'

Danny also stood up, looking sheepish. He was more stocky than fat, Tessa thought.

'I'll just say a few words about what we do here for the two of you who are new. Then we'll push on with the weigh-in.'

Weigh-in. The phrase made them sound like a fishing catch, and Tessa felt blubbery enough as it was. She didn't like Janice, the thin woman who was talking to them, she was too bossy by half, and the man called Bill was smiling too much, as if he was only pretending he was pleased to be there.

Tessa only half-listened to the talk about the Will To Be Slim and Sensible Eating. It was just what she'd expected. It made her think of being in church. They were treating slimming like it was a religion and they wanted to convert you to it because only the slim and beautiful could find true happiness. It was depressing. Yet it was also kind of comforting, and Tessa found herself wanting to be thin more than ever, and wanting to please Janice and Bill.

She stood behind Danny in the weigh-in queue and was grateful for the seven pounds she'd already lost. As she stood on the scales, she thought she caught a tut of disapproval from Janice, and a look of pity from Bill, but she couldn't be sure. When everyone had been weighed, there was a round of applause for the ones who'd lost weight, while the ones who'd gained were told not to be discouraged and that Rome wasn't built in a day, but that they would need to exercise more of that will-power if they were going to turn into the slim little person that was trying to get out of their round little bodies. Tessa noticed that they used the word little a lot.

Then they were each summoned for a little personal chat about their likes and dislikes when it came to food and what they would find it hardest to give up. Tessa said chocolate when she spoke to Janice; she couldn't stop eating it. So she was given a diet sheet which allowed her a Mars or a twin Milky Way or a Kit Kat every single day. 'And I can eat this and still get slim?' asked Tessa incredulously.

'That's right,' said Janice, with a look of amusement. 'You thought you'd have to give up all your favourite things, didn't you? Well, let me tell you, slimming isn't all pain and denial you know. It can be fun, too.'

Tessa doubted that she would ever find the path to thinness fun, but at least there was chocolate to be picked up along the way, and that was something. She stopped disliking Janice quite so much, and felt hopeful again as she went to sit with the others.

The children who'd been attending the slimming club for a long time were asked to say something about why they'd decided to lose weight and what slimming had done for them. Lucy spoke first. She said, 'I wanted to lose weight because all my life I have been too fat. Chinese people are usually so slim and I didn't want to be different. Now people don't stare at me so much when I go out with my friends. I can wear jeans. I like the diet, it's fine. I don't eat so many cakes and my skin looks nicer too.'

Lucy sat down shyly at the end of her little speech. Tessa liked her and wished they could be friends. It would be good to know someone who understood what it was like to be fat. And it would be good to have a friend who was a girl because girls understood things that boys just didn't have to think about.

Then Gemma stood up and said when she was fat, nobody wanted to know her, but since she'd lost weight, she'd become the most popular girl in her class. She seemed thrilled to bits that she'd made so many new friends, but Tessa began to wonder about it. Could you really want to be friends with people who'd laughed at you for months and months because they thought you didn't look as nice as they did? Tessa tried to imagine being friendly with Sonia once she was thin and decided it would be impossible.

Gemma seemed really pleased with herself. 'And I've come to realize that you can do anything if only you believe you can,' she said with a sweet little smile. Tessa felt like puking, and decided Gemma was someone to avoid. She'd be first in line to call other people fatty now, Tessa could tell. She had such a smug look about her, and she was going on and on about wanting to help others who were less fortunate than she had been. Yuck and double yuck. Tessa was glad she wasn't sitting anywhere near the little creep.

'Well,' said Janice with a smile, 'I think that just about wraps it up for this week. Thank you for coming, everyone. And don't forget, it's all a matter of will-power and determination, so keep up the good work. See you all next Monday. Goodbye for now.' Janice and Bill left the podium with a flourish. Tessa half expected everyone to clap, but instead they filed out quietly into the street.

'It was good, wasn't it?' said Joy. 'One of the mothers told me it's an idea that's come from America. They even have slimming camps over there for the kids. Janice and Bill went over to see how it all worked and came back full of enthusiasm.'

'I thought it was terrible,' growled Tessa.

'Does that mean you won't be giving it a go?'

127

Tessa thought for a moment. She hadn't liked Gemma, but she'd liked the idea of wearing leggings and a big, baggy jumper, and there was a lot she was prepared to do to make that possible. 'I'll have to think about it,' she answered cautiously, but this was enough for her mother.

'You'll be happier once you've lost that weight, won't you, love?' she said.

Tessa nodded, though for the first time there was a tiny doubt in her mind. What if being thin wasn't all it was cracked up to be? What if it didn't make everything all right? Tessa pushed the horrible suggestion from her mind and hurried past the chip shop.

14

Jasper was sitting by the window in the front room, waiting for Tessa. He was planning to take the lift to the ground floor as soon as he saw her approaching the tower block. Then he could bring her up to the flat and show her everything properly.

Every now and then he glanced around the room, trying to see it with Tessa's eyes. Perhaps she would find the curtains too bright, and she was bound to notice that an area near the corner was painted a shade darker than the rest of the wall. The crack in the kitchen ceiling was all too visible and the gas cooker was old-fashioned and too big. In the bathroom, the toilet seat was likely to eject you if you didn't sit down carefully enough. How could you warn someone about a thing like that? Jasper tried to puzzle it out, but soon gave up. And what about his bedroom? It was so small you could only just get a bed in it and a chest of drawers. And his bedspread was Mr Men – no one of nearly twelve had Mr Men in their room any more, it was just asking to be laughed at.

He peered out of the window, concentrating hard. A girl who might have been Tessa hurried into the building, but Jasper could tell by her walk that it wasn't his friend. He looked at the clock on the mantelpiece. She was ten minutes late. What if she had changed her mind and decided not to come? His mother had baked some special cakes and there was tinned salmon in the sandwiches. It would be wasted if Tessa didn't turn up. And then his mother would be furious to think they'd splashed out like that for nothing. Tinned salmon, the red variety, was expensive and she wouldn't have bought it, only he had begged and begged her to let them have something special for tea. He'd feel so stupid if Tessa stood him up now, after the way he'd carried on about making everything nice.

Jasper thought again about how he'd had to force himself to ask Tess to come. He'd practised saying the words for days in the quiet of his bedroom. Then finally he'd said them out loud at break time on Thursday morning, and Tessa had answered, 'Sure, if you like', not 'I'll think about it', or 'Maybe', but a definite yes.

As he was remembering, Jasper kept his eyes on the grass verge leading to the flats, and suddenly he saw her; she was actually moving along the path, half walking, half running and wearing her blue anorak, the one with the red flowers on. She wasn't allowed to put it on for school, she always kept it for best, which meant that Tessa felt that coming to see him, Jasper, was a special thing to do, something to wear your nicest clothes for. He felt so proud he almost forgot to dash downstairs to meet her.

He was just in time; he came out of the lift as she was preparing to get in it. 'Hiya,' he said.

'Where are you going?' she asked.

He didn't know if it was all right to be so eager

that he'd been coming to meet her, so he just looked bashful and muttered something that didn't make a lot of sense. Tessa grinned and said, 'Are we going up again, then?' so he stopped the lift doors closing and they went up in it to the eleventh floor.

'I wasn't sure what you would like for tea. Do you like salmon? My mum's made a raisin cake and I got some ginger beer, only if you'd rather have Coke, I could go and get some. We only have a black and white TV, but there isn't really anything good on anyway so it won't matter much. We could go out if you don't want to stay in all the time. There's not much to do round here though, there isn't a park and on the estate there's only a ramp for skateboarding only I haven't got a skateboard —'

The lift door opened. Jasper stepped out, and Tessa followed. 'It's OK, Jasper,' she said, 'whatever you want to do is fine.' Tessa was touched by his nervousness. No one had wanted to please her this much before. It gave her a good feeling.

In the front room the table was already laid with an African print tablecloth. Jasper's mother came in. 'Hello, Tessa darling,' she said, and she put down a plate of home-made cakes.

'They look lovely,' said Tessa, forgetting for a moment that she was on a diet.

'Jasper wanted something special,' said his mother, causing him to squirm.

Tessa went over to the window. 'You've got a lovely view,' she said.

Jasper joined her. 'If you look over there, you can see Big Ben and the River Thames. And across there you can see St Paul's.'

'It's brilliant,' said Tessa.

'There's a balcony. Shall I open the door? We could go outside.'

'No, Jasper, you know how that door sticks,' said his mother. 'Besides, it's starting to rain.'

Jasper stopped pulling at the door and came back into the middle of the room, looking disappointed. 'It's nearly tea-time, anyway,' he said.

'How's your mother, Tessa?' said Mrs Woodrow.

'Fine, thanks.'

'I sometimes see her when I go to the chemist. I don't think she recognizes me though, we only met the once.'

'You should tell her who you are,' said Tessa politely.

'Maybe next time,' she answered. 'Jasper, fetch the sandwiches from the kitchen and pour a drink for Tessa.'

Jasper disappeared and Tessa sat on the settee. As she looked round the room, she noticed that the paint in the corner didn't match the rest of the paintwork on the walls. It didn't matter though. It was cosy in this flat, she decided, and she felt welcome. She wished Jasper and his mum would relax a bit though, they were starting to make her nervous.

Jasper returned with two glasses of ginger beer. Tessa calculated that the one glass would have at least a hundred calories in it. She couldn't refuse it, though, it wouldn't be polite. She sipped it very slowly; if she could make it last, she wouldn't have to drink another one and that would be a lot of calories saved.

'How do you like school now, Tessa?' asked Jasper's mum.

Tessa wondered if an honest answer would be acceptable and then decided to risk it. 'I utterly hate it,' she said.

Mrs Woodrow laughed. 'I think Jasper feels the same, though he does like lessons, strange boy.'

Tessa could understand this though. 'It's good fun, being able to do things and not finding them hard when everyone else does.' Tessa was trying to say that she liked lessons too because being good at them was a way of getting even with her classmates — she could show them up in much the same way as they showed her up in games. They might be thin, but she was smart; she had the edge in one thing at least.

Jasper said, 'I like finding out about things and being able to make sense of them. It's interesting. Would you like tea now, or would you rather wait a bit?'

They decided to eat. Tessa sat at the table and wished she'd had the strength of mind to refuse the invitation to visit Jasper's home. It wasn't that she didn't want to see him, it was just that she couldn't say no to the food on the table without disappointing them. She could see they'd gone to a lot of trouble. But once she started eating a full meal, she feared it would be like an avalanche and she'd want to go on and on stuffing herself and never stop. She reached for the salmon sandwiches.

They were delicious. It was no good, she was doomed to fatness and a cringe-making session with Janice and Bill at the weigh-in on Monday.

At last Tessa sat back, uncomfortably full and facing a table of empty plates. Jasper's mother began to clear them away. Tessa stood up and piled some of the crockery ready to take it into the kitchen.

'It's all right, Tessa, Jasper will see to it.'

Jasper jumped up in readiness. 'I'll help him,' said Tessa. 'It won't take long if two of us do it.'

Tessa carried the glasses and cutlery while Jasper took the plates to the kitchen. She filled a sink full of water and found the washing-up liquid. She remembered how she'd enjoyed playing with the bubbles as a little kid. Her dad had bought her a bubble kit in the end, with proper liquid, the kind that you could blow into massive bubbles that reflected rainbow colours. It was a pity anyone ever had to grow up. Her thoughts were too young for her big balloon shape, and she wished she could get used to having such a huge body.

'What's the matter, Tess?' asked Jasper nervously as he dried the dishes.

'Nothing.'

'Yes, there is, tell me what it is.'

'I've broken my diet. It's hopeless, I'll never be thin.'

'You will if you want to, Tess, I'm sure you will. I should have asked Mum for some diet food, only I forgot, I thought you'd like the salmon and the cake.'

Tessa hadn't wanted him to be disappointed, so she

said, 'The trouble was, Jasper, I liked them too much. I ate everything because it tasted so good.'

Jasper smiled. 'You can diet extra hard tomorrow,' he said.

Tessa nodded. Tomorrow was always a better prospect than today. She'd just eat fruit and crispbread all day, and then she'd be 'on course for a thinner future', as Janice would have put it.

'What do you want to do now?' said Jasper.

'What is there?'

'I could show you my maps, if you like.'

Tessa nodded, sensing that Jasper's maps were important to him and that he wanted her to understand about them.

Jasper took her into his bedroom and got out a big folder which he spread out over his bed. 'They're maps of all the places I'm going to visit when I'm grown-up. I've got travel brochures too and names of all the airlines that let you fly cheap. I'm saving up. When I'm eighteen, I'll have at least a hundred pounds. They let you fly cheaper if you're a student, so I'll go on some trips when I'm at university.'

Tessa calculated how long it would be before Jasper was eighteen. Seven years, probably. That was an awful long time. It was hard to imagine him grown up. 'Will you have a beard?' she said, trying to picture what he would be like.

'A moustache,' he answered. 'And I'll have the best trainers, those really expensive black ones we saw down Market Street.'

'Where will you go first?'

'Jamaica.'

Tessa knew why he wanted to go there. It was where his family was from. 'I'm going there too,' Tessa said. 'My grandparents went back four years ago. They said I could come on a visit as soon as I'm old enough. If you don't have anywhere else to stay, you could come with me.'

Jasper's face took on an expression of pure pleasure. '*Really?*'

'Of course,' Tessa said. 'The beaches have white sand. It's better than anywhere, better than Bournemouth or Brighton. It's even better than Southend. And it's 25 degrees Celsius even on a cold day. And then there are the markets where you can buy practically anything really cheap, and they sell fish straight from the sea, things like lobsters, I expect. Have you ever tasted lobster?'

Jasper shook his head.

'I did once, when I was with Dad. It's excellent, you'd really like it . . .' Tessa faltered for a moment, thinking about the diet. It wouldn't take her seven years to get slim. She comforted herself with the thought that she'd be able to eat anything she wanted by then. 'And I'll tell you something else. In Jamaica, people are much more friendly than they are here. I bet we'd have lots of friends if we went. People would really like us. Show me the brochure. I want to see where we could visit when we went there. Do they have any pictures of the Blue Mountains? I tell you what, I could buy a really big map and we could put pins in it for where we want to go. What do you think, Jasper? Would you do it with me? It would be brilliant, wouldn't it?'

Jasper nodded, thinking that brilliant was a bit of an understatement. If Tessa was thinking about being with him when they were grown-up, it must mean that they were really friends, the best sort of friends you could get. 'Yes, we'll buy a big map,' he said quietly, and turned over the pages of the brochure, imagining flying with Tessa in an aeroplane to the beaches of Jamaica.

15

Tessa spread the map out in front of her on her bedroom floor. There was Jamaica . . . Her finger traced some of the other Caribbean islands: Trinidad, Barbados, Haiti . . . She imagined being there with Jasper, finding all the places where their ancestors had lived, and walking along the wind-swept beaches. They would swim in a clear sea and watch fish from glass-bottomed boats. Tessa sighed. She wanted to be in another place in much the same way as she wanted to be in another body. Going away was a dream, like being thin and beautiful. She folded up the maps and pushed them under her bed.

'Tessa, have you finished tidying your room yet?' called Joy.

'Nearly.'

'Get a move on, will you? Your meeting starts in three-quarters of an hour.'

Tessa opened a cupboard and crammed two pairs of battered trainers into the last remaining space. She caught sight of herself in the mirror, and looked at her reflection anxiously. She'd lost another three pounds that week, and it had to show somewhere. Were her arms thinner, or her legs? Maybe soon she'd be able to get a tracksuit. You had to be thin to wear the kind she was thinking of. It would be bright green with a thin black stripe down the sides of the legs. The top would be shorter than the sort she usually wore because it wouldn't be so important to hide her massive thighs. She'd look . . . fit.

The three or four other black kids in her class at school (not counting Jasper, of course) wouldn't be seen dead in the clothes she usually wore. They were sharp dressers, with pretty faces and long skinny legs . . . and that was just the boys, Tessa added to herself, with a little grin.

It would be truly amazingly wonderful if she could belong more. She'd have the kind of trainers Martin wore and she'd look so smart he'd have to notice her. Sonia was just a phase with him. And the girls would include her all the time, and they'd go round the shopping centre together, trying on clothes and makeup and just hanging out looking sharp and cool . . . And Sonia would hurry past them with her head down knowing that she could never join Tessa's posse, because Tessa only had the most beautiful people in it, and they had to be nice as well.

'Are you ready yet, Tess?'

'Nearly.'

Tessa opened her wardrobe and put a skirt inside it. The clothes that were hanging there were just embarrassing. No wonder nobody wanted to know her. She pulled out a thin cotton dress for the meeting at the slimming club. It was drab, but it was very light, and it wouldn't add to her weight at weigh-in time. As she pulled it over her head, she looked at her stomach. Flatter than last week, definitely. One day (maybe) she'd be able to wear a belt without looking like a sack of potatoes.

'Are you coming, Tessa?'

'In a minute, Mum,' she said.

They were only five minutes late for the meeting and several others weren't there yet. Tessa didn't see any parents apart from her own mother. They'd all dropped out weeks ago.

'Look, Mum, couldn't you go back home?'

'Don't you want me here then?'

'No one else has their parents with them any more. Lucy's mother's gone off with some of the others to wait in the café over the road. Couldn't you go with them? Please. I don't want to be the only one. I am nearly twelve.'

'If that's what you want,' said Joy coldly.

'Thanks, Mum. See you later.'

Tessa joined the others. They didn't sit in rows any more, they sat in a circle. Janice said it helped them to talk more freely about their diets. Tessa had managed to avoid speaking so far. She didn't want to have to say all kinds of personal stuff in front of everyone. It was embarrassing; even the thought made her feel creepy.

'You sent your mum packing then,' said Lucy.

'You bet. She thinks I'm still a little kid.' They laughed at the absurdity of it.

'How much do you think you've lost this week?'

'About three pounds.'

'That's brilliant. I'm stuck. Janice says that after a bit, you reach a plateau and you don't lose any weight for a while however much you stick to the diet. Then it all starts dropping again. So I'm trying not to feel too bad, or to worry about it.'

'You've done so well though.'

'I can wear size ten now. Trouble is, I'm short, so I've still got a few pounds to go. I've decided to cut down to six or seven hundred calories a day. Don't tell anyone though, we're not supposed to do that.'

'I won't tell. You look really slim though. I wish I was you.'

Lucy grinned self-consciously. 'You'll get there in the end,' she said. 'We all will. Anyway, I'm fatter than you.'

'Don't be stupid.'

'I am though. I don't weigh so much but I look much bigger. It shows more on me.'

Tessa thought about it. She wanted it to be true, but she knew that it wasn't. Lucy was looking even slimmer than a normal person. Why didn't she see it for herself? Tessa sighed and said, 'It would be nice, wouldn't it, if no one ever had to go on a diet and it didn't matter how fat or thin you were because everybody liked you anyway.'

'Nobody likes fat people,' said Lucy sadly.

'I know. I was just wishing.'

'Lucy and Tessa, there's too much whispering going on. Why don't you share it with the rest of us?' said Janice.

Tessa shook her head. It was just like school at the club in some ways, with people checking up on you with weigh-ins and all that, and having to behave properly all the time.

The meeting finished early because Janice had to go

to give a talk on children and dieting somewhere after-wards. 'My mum won't be back for nearly half an hour yet,' said Tessa. 'She's gone with your mum to the café.'

'I bet they're having cake,' said Lucy.

'Chocolate cake.'

'Lemon cake with icing.'

'French fries.'

'Milkshakes.'

'Double cheeseburgers. Let's not even think about it,' Tessa said.

'No, let's not,' said Lucy. 'They're closing the hall. We'll have to go. I don't want to sit with Mum in that café though, it'll be too tempting.'

'I know. Me neither.'

'What shall we do then?'

'Let's just go for a walk. It'll be good for us. It will burn some calories.'

'That's true,' said Lucy happily.

It was a warm evening in early spring. Tessa pictured herself in a cotton jacket with a fitted waist. One day, perhaps . . . Lucy was already thin enough to wear anything she pleased, but she was still covering herself up in a baggy sweatshirt and loose jeans. Tessa shortened her pace so that Lucy could keep up. She was small and neat-looking. Now that she was slim, her lack of height seemed more noticeable. She looked fragile to Tessa, and in need of protection.

'Maybe we should walk faster,' said Lucy after a while. 'It uses more calories.'

Tessa speeded up. Lucy's shorter legs had to move so

quickly that she was almost running now, but she didn't seem to mind. 'I wish I hadn't eaten so much breakfast,' she said.

'What did you have?'

'An orange and two pieces of toast.'

'With butter?'

Lucy looked horrified at the mere idea. 'No, toast by itself.'

'What about lunch?'

'I skipped that. Well, I did eat some grapes. Just five or six.'

'You mean that's all you've had all day, two slices of toast, an orange and six grapes?'

Lucy nodded.

'How do you do it? I mean, I don't have the will-power, nothing like.'

'It's hard, but it's worth it. I just think about being thin one day.'

'Me too,' said Tessa. 'Everything's nicer when you're thin, isn't it? Sometimes I think that if I hadn't let myself get so fat, everything would be different at home.'

'What do you mean?'

'Maybe my dad would have stayed home if I'd looked better . . . all that.'

'Oh,' said Lucy. 'Does he like girls to be thin then?'

'I think so. It seemed like that at Christmas when we were watching TV.'

'Oh,' said Lucy again. 'Everybody's thin in my family. Much thinner than me.'

'My mother's thin. Well, you've seen her. And my sister. She's only a size eight, and she's quite tall. I have this friend called Jasper. Well, not really a friend . . .'

'A boyfriend?'

'No! I mean, he's a boy, but you couldn't call him a boyfriend, it would be stupid. Anyway, we had this club for people who didn't fit – they were too fat or wore thick glasses or whatever. He called it the Misfits Club . . .'

'What about it?' said Lucy after a few moments' silence.

'Oh, nothing really,' said Tessa. How could you explain? Tessa wanted two contrary things at once. On the one hand, she wanted to be different, and to be Jasper's friend, and to think about going places with him when they were grown-up. But on the other hand she wanted to be normal, to fit in with everybody, and to be thin. She'd been trying to find a way of asking Lucy if she felt muddled about changing herself, and how she thought of herself now she'd lost weight. But it was too hard to put it into words. It was good walking with Lucy though. She understood things, and she was nice. That was the thing about being thinner. It was easier to have friends when you weren't a barrage balloon. People liked you better.

16

Tessa and Jasper stood on the concourse at Victoria Station and scanned the departure board. The Brighton train was due to leave from platform eighteen in fifteen minutes. 'Have you got your tickets safely?' asked Joy, pushing a sachet of tissues into Tessa's hand.

'Yes, Mum,' she answered for the fourth time, bored now with the question.

'And you know exactly where you're meeting your dad?'

'At the ticket barrier as we get off the train.'

'And you won't talk to anyone or let anyone except your dad take you anywhere?'

'What about the man who checks your ticket on the train? Can't I speak to him?' asked Tessa. She knew full well what her mother meant, but it was more fun if she pretended that she hadn't understood.

'Don't be silly, Tessa,' said Joy.

'Can we get on the train now? All the best seats will have gone. We want one with a table so that we can play cards on it.'

They began to walk towards platform eighteen. 'Perhaps I should be going with you as this is your first visit. There's no one to cover me though, at the dispensary, now that Andy Moon is off sick.'

'Andy Moon?' said Jasper, too busy looking at trains

to give the conversation his full attention. It was a good name, that, the sort of name you could write a poem or a song about.

'We'll be fine, Mum. How could we get lost just being on a train from here to Brighton station? Don't worry so much.'

'Let's get in this one,' said Jasper, opening the carriage door.

Joy followed them up the step. 'Where will you sit?'

'Here,' said Jasper, sliding on to the window seat and gesturing towards the one opposite for Tessa. He put his belongings carefully on the empty seat beside him to stop any other passengers from joining them.

Tessa brought out a tube of fruit-flavoured Polos and a deck of cards. She began to shuffle them. 'We're all right, Mum, honest. You can go now.'

Joy laughed. 'Sounds as if you can't wait to get rid of me.'

Tessa shuffled the cards again to hide her discomfort. She did want her mother to go because she wanted to begin the journey. This was a very long goodbye and they were running out of things to say. Why couldn't her mother just get off to work? All this fussing about everything wasn't necessary.

Joy kissed her cheek and put a hand lightly on Jasper's shoulder. 'Phone me tonight, OK? Don't forget, or I'll be worried. And tell your dad –'

There was a loud buzz and then a voice came over the Tannoy: 'Good morning, ladies and gentlemen, this is the eight thirty-nine service from London Victoria to

Brighton. We will be departing shortly. Passengers are advised that the buffet will be open in five minutes and will be serving both English and Continental breakfasts . . .'

'What's a Continental breakfast?' asked Jasper.

' 'Bye, Mum,' said Tessa with an impatient wave. 'Continental breakfasts are croissants with jam and stuff . . . you know.'

'I'd rather have bacon.'

'Well, you can't. We've got a carton of fruit juice each and a bun to have on the journey. Anyway, they cost a fortune, breakfasts on trains.' Tessa's mother was standing on the platform, peering in at them through the window. 'I wish she'd go now,' said Tessa, catching sight of her.

'Mothers worry,' said Jasper. 'Are you going to deal those cards now, or what?'

They'd chosen a slow train. After three games of gin rummy and a drink and a bun, they were still only at Redhill. 'I wish this train would hurry up,' said Tessa.

'I quite like it,' said Jasper. 'This is only the seventh or eighth time I've ever been on a train. I wouldn't mind train-spotting.'

'Kid's stuff,' said Tessa with scorn.

'You see grown-ups doing it,' answered Jasper.

'Only pathetic grown-ups in stretchy trousers and dirty parkas.'

'I still think it would be interesting,' said Jasper stubbornly. 'It would be a bit like maps.'

'How do you make that out?'

'It's to do with journeys, isn't it? Do you want another game?'

'Not rummy. Do you know anything else?'

'Pontoon.'

'You mean twenty-ones? It's not very good with only two.'

'Poker.'

'You can play poker? Honest?'

'My cousins taught me. I should think you could play it with only two people, I'm not sure. You don't always have to play for money, you can use matchsticks.'

'We don't have any.'

'We could buy some.'

'Not if all we're going to do is bet with them. It would be a waste.'

'What do you want to play then?' said Jasper, beginning to feel fed up with having all his suggestions turned down.

'Let's just look out of the window,' said Tessa. She slumped in her seat and began to drum against the table with her foot. Jasper took out a computer magazine and began to read.

'What's the time?' asked Tessa after a few minutes.

'You know I haven't got a watch,' said Jasper.

'Do you think we're nearly there?'

'I don't know. Not yet. It takes a lot more than an hour on the slow train, I heard a man saying that.'

'Could we have missed our stop while we were playing cards?'

'No,' said Jasper. 'Brighton's a terminus. There isn't

any more track for the train to go on. It's always the last stop, like Victoria.'

'Just testing,' said Tessa, wishing she hadn't displayed her ignorance quite so obviously. 'OK, let's play cards again then.'

They played two more hands and then ran out of interest. Tessa got up to go to the toilet. Jasper watched her moving down the train and noticed that her jeans had gone from being stretched tight across her thighs to being baggy enough to fit two people. The diet must be working then. It was the first time he'd noticed. As she returned to her seat, Jasper noticed more. Her arms were thinner too, and her face was less round and childish. Tessa was looking like she was thirteen or more. They entered a tunnel with a sudden rush, and Jasper saw his reflection gleaming strongly in the darkened window. He still looked nine. People would think he was four years younger at least. No wonder he was treated like a little boy whenever they went out together.

'Wake up, Jasper. I said, do you want another Polo?'

'No thanks.'

'Me neither. I don't know why I bought them really. They've got loads of sugar in them.'

'Are you still dieting?' asked Jasper, though he knew the answer.

'I've lost a lot,' said Tessa proudly. 'There's this girl at the slimming club called Lucy, and she looks really different now. I went round to her house last week. Her mum cooked us low-calorie Chinese food. It was excellent.'

'You didn't tell me.'

'I don't have to tell you everything, Jasper Woodrow.'

Jasper sighed. It was true, Tessa didn't have to tell him everything, but he felt that it was a sign that she had other interests now, other friends. If she really got to like this Lucy, would she still want him to hang around, or would she get fed up? 'Do you want the other half of my bun?' he said.

'No,' said Tessa firmly.

She never ate his food these days, she stuck with her own. It depressed Jasper to think that they didn't share any more.

'Why are you looking so miserable?' Tessa demanded.

'I'm not. Let's play another game,' Jasper answered.

'We can't,' said Tessa. 'I think we're there.'

The train slid slowly into Brighton station. Tessa wished they could open a window to see better, but you couldn't do that any more. They pushed impatiently at the button that opened the doors and at last they parted. Tessa and Jasper rushed through them, happy to escape.

Brighton station was old-fashioned but newly painted. As they hurried towards the ticket barrier, Jasper wrinkled his nose and sniffed. 'I can smell the sea,' he said.

Tessa stopped and sniffed too, but she couldn't smell anything apart from the grime of the trains and the freshly cooked burgers that were sold in the station café. 'There's Dad,' she said suddenly, and ran to him. As she did so, she became aware of how much more easily she could move now that she had lost some weight. Her jeans were miles too big and she was wearing a smaller bra. She hoped that Paul would notice how much better she looked, and be proud of her.

'Tessa!' He swept her into his arms and as she felt his warmth, she realized how much she had missed him. It was more than three weeks since he had moved, and this was the first visit. Whatever Joy might say, he had gone far away and things were not the same.

'Hi there, Jasper,' said Paul, pausing to greet him. 'Had your hair cut?'

Jasper nodded. 'I don't like it, it's too short.'

'It looks fine to me. And it will soon grow.'

'What about me, Dad? How do I look?'

'Beautiful as ever, Tess,' he said.

'No, seriously, Dad. What's different about me?'

He laughed uncomfortably. 'You know I'm no good at this, Tess. Tell me what it is.'

'No, you have to guess. It's obvious.'

Paul moved back a few paces to get a better look. He continued to stare.

'She's lost weight,' said Jasper loudly. He couldn't stand the thought that Paul wouldn't see it and Tessa would be disappointed.

'Of course she has, I was just about to say that. Those jeans are hanging off you, Tess.'

'You shouldn't have told,' Tessa hissed at Jasper. 'You're such a fool sometimes.'

'I am not,' said Jasper crossly.

'You knew I wanted him to guess it by himself.'

Paul took Tessa's bag and Jasper's backpack. 'Come

on, they'll give me a ticket if we don't hurry up. I could see you'd lost weight, Tess, it was the first thing I noticed, but I wasn't sure if that was what you wanted me to see. I mean, you're wearing new shoes, aren't you? And your hair is plaited differently.'

Tessa was soothed a little by this. She stopped glaring at Jasper and began to chat about the film they'd seen the previous week.

'Can we look at the sea first?' asked Jasper as they got into the car.

'I thought we could go to a café on the sea front and have some cake.'

'No, Dad,' said Tessa.

'Don't you want to?' asked Paul in surprise.

'No.'

'It interferes with the diet,' said Jasper, feeling the need to explain things once more.

'Shut up, Jasper,' said Tessa sharply.

'Sorry, Tess,' said Paul. 'I forgot about the diet. We won't bother with anything before lunch. Unless you'd like something, Jasper?'

'He wouldn't,' said Tessa.

Paul laughed. 'Let him speak for himself, darling.'

'I wouldn't,' said Jasper. It was the only possible answer.

'We could still take a look at the sea though, couldn't we, Dad?' said Tessa.

'I don't see why not,' said Paul.

It was only a few minutes' drive to the sea from the station – they barely had time to fasten their seatbelts.

Tessa had been to Brighton before, so she knew it wasn't a proper sandy beach but one that was covered in sharp little pebbles. They walked down to the front and gazed at the murky water which seemed to merge so completely with the grey sky that there was no horizon.

'I wish it was blue,' said Jasper.

'It is a bit dull at the moment,' said Paul, 'but they've forecast sunshine for this afternoon. It's misty. You often get sea mists here.'

'I don't mind it grey,' said Tessa, concerned that their reaction was a disappointment to him. She could tell that her father wanted them to like his new surroundings. 'What's on the pier?' she said.

'Would you like to go on it?' said her father, for once picking up his cue.

'I wouldn't mind,' chorused Tessa and Jasper together.

You didn't even have to pay to walk on the pier, and as far as Tessa was concerned, it was brilliant. If you looked down at the wooden slats, you could see the sea glittering coldly beneath you. Children ran up and down while elderly couples strolled slowly, arm in arm, remembering what it used to be like in the old days before people took their holidays abroad. It smelled of fish and chips mixed with the overpowering sweetness of candyfloss and fresh-cooked doughnuts which were arranged in trays and dusted with powdery sugar. Tessa went over to stare at them longingly. Damn the diet, she said to herself, half expecting to be struck down for swearing. Life was so unfair. Why couldn't her dad have moved

153

before she started getting thin? Then she could have eaten all the delights she wanted and not be left with this hollow craving inside of her.

There was an amusement arcade up ahead, and Tessa and Jasper hurried inside, drawn by the discordant beeps and buzzes and the flashing lights. Paul dug into his pocket and gave them each a handful of coins. Jasper found a machine which hooked him at once. You put your money in and these funny-looking creatures popped out of their holes. In order to score, you had to bang them on the head before they ducked out of sight. Jasper couldn't get enough of it, he seemed to be mesmerized by these creatures, and it was such fun to be vicious and to bash them as hard as you could, knowing all the while that you weren't really doing any harm. You could really let yourself go, thought Jasper, and get rid of all the crossness that had ever been inside you. It occurred to Jasper that he had actually been cross for quite a long time without realizing it. He was cross with Tessa for getting thinner and finding new friends, and he was cross with himself for being short and having buck teeth and needing to wear glasses.

'I just got four ten pence pieces!' said Tessa, appearing beside him. 'You have to put a ten pence in and then the machine pushes a whole pile of them to the edge. If yours falls in the right place, the others are knocked through the hole and you can have them. Come and see.'

'I want to do this,' said Jasper, with unusual firmness.

'You're getting quite violent,' said Tessa, after watching for a moment or two.

'It doesn't really hurt them,' said Jasper absently.

'I know that, I'm not stupid, a baby could tell you that.'

'It doesn't matter if I hit them hard then, does it?'

Tessa shrugged. Jasper was being argumentative and it wasn't like him at all. Maybe the sea air was getting to him. Or maybe he was hungry. It was long past lunch. She turned to her father and said, 'Dad, can we have our lunch here on the pier?'

'If you like. What do you want to eat? There's quite a lot to choose from.'

'Fish and chips,' said Jasper.

'No,' said Tessa. 'It's too fattening.' She looked close to tears, caught between longing to eat them and longing to be thin.

'Why not forget about the diet just for one day, Tess? It's not worth being upset about,' said Paul.

'I can't, they have a weigh-in. If you haven't stuck to the diet, everybody knows.'

'We could have jacket potatoes without butter. They do cottage cheese. That doesn't make you put on weight. My mum ate that all the time when she did her diet,' said Jasper.

'How about sharing some fish and chips with me, Tess?' said Paul. 'Then you wouldn't need to eat so much.'

'No. I wouldn't stop, you know I wouldn't. I'd end up eating them all.'

'Can't you just have a nice day, Tess? Otherwise, it's a bit miserable for me and Jasper.'

155

'Not half as miserable as it is for me. You can eat what you like, and you're not fat!'

'Look, here's some money. Take it and get what you want. It's up to you. We'll all sit in these deckchairs and eat what we've each bought. Here you are, Jasper, this is yours.'

'My mum gave me some money.'

'That's OK, you're our guest. Off you go. And I don't want to hear another word about diets, OK?'

Tessa ran off silently. When she returned with Jasper, they each had a bag of chips and a piece of fish, lightly salted and wet with vinegar. Paul didn't say anything, but he looked relieved as he went to fetch some for himself.

At the far end of the pier there was a ghost train, a helter-skelter and some dodgems. They looked old; the paint was peeling and they weren't big rides, or exciting ones like you found at theme parks. Still, they were better than nothing, Tessa decided.

'Hadn't you better wait until your meal's had a chance to settle, you two?'

'No, we'll be fine, Dad,' said Tessa.

And it was more fun than she'd expected, sitting in the ghost train and feeling cobwebs brush your face and seeing these pretty pathetic skeletons covered in luminous paint dangling over your head.

'Do you want to go again?' she said to Jasper, when the ride stopped.

'It was excellent,' he said, so they didn't get out of the carriage, they just paid the man again and went straight back in.

'What would you like to do tomorrow?' asked Paul as they wandered back towards the car.

'Swim in the sea,' said Jasper.

'Too cold,' said Paul. 'You'll catch pneumonia and your mother will think that being a doctor, I should have seen it coming.'

Jasper grinned. 'But I've never swum in the sea,' he said.

'It's too polluted here anyway,' said Tessa. She wasn't ready to be seen in a swimsuit, she was still miles too fat, and if she couldn't do it, she didn't see why Jasper should be allowed to.

'Maybe another time,' said Paul. 'When it's warmer. You'll be here again soon. You could try it then.'

Jasper sighed. All the good things you ever wanted to do got put off for another time. Still, at least Paul was expecting him to come here again with Tessa. That must mean he was almost part of the family. The idea gave Jasper such a good feeling that he forgot what he was doing and grabbed Tessa's hand. They walked together for a while. Tessa seemed not to mind, and Jasper's joy increased, but then suddenly she pulled away and began to run ahead, leaving him with this terrible sense that she wasn't merely running for the sake of it, she was running away from him.

It was as if it had suddenly started snowing on a hot day. Jasper began to run after Tessa as he always did, hoping it was just their usual game, but he could tell from the way she moved, without once looking back, that she didn't want him to follow her. He slowed down to a walk and tried to pretend that he didn't mind what she did, it was all the same to him. And anyway, he told himself, at least they were at the seaside, and at least they were going to the pictures that evening. And it wasn't really cold at all, it wasn't even raining.

17

Jasper stared out of the classroom window and looked across the playing fields. The lesson was boring – he knew all that stuff anyway, about how volcanoes worked, he'd known it for years. So it really didn't matter if he bothered to listen or not.

There was a stiff breeze that shook the trees and sent the clouds scudding across a grey-blue sky. It reminded Jasper of the time he'd spent in Brighton with Tess. He began to chew on his pencil, causing little fragments of wood to splinter in his mouth.

Whenever Jasper looked back at that weekend in Brighton, he remembered it as the last time he'd been really happy. It had been so good, walking along the promenade, holding Tessa's hand and feeling there was someone (apart from his mother) who really liked him and wanted to be with him whatever he looked like and however young for his age he was. And then without any warning, Tessa had shaken him off and had run ahead as if she had been trying to get away from him. Jasper licked his lips and tried not to let the memory make him too miserable. He wondered how he'd got through the rest of that day, and then he remembered that for a while he'd pretended that it hadn't happened. He'd told himself that he'd got it wrong, and that Tessa hadn't meant it like that, and then he'd pushed it out of

159

his mind. It was easier to forget it and to try to enjoy himself again, and he'd managed it, right until the end of the visit. The miniature railway had helped.

Paul's new house overlooked the sea, and from the window in the spare bedroom you could see a miniature railway that had real trains running along the coast. You could actually ride on them, and the next day they'd had a go and it had been awesome, sitting in the front of a train that chugged along the sea front and had wooden seats and was painted brown and yellow. You could feel the sea air blowing round you and smell the salt, and you went past a beach where people were allowed to bathe without any clothes on. They'd really laughed when they'd seen two bald men waddling about completely bare. It had been brilliant.

Then, on the journey home, he and Tessa had told each other stories about the places they would visit when they were grown up and could do whatever they liked without ever being told off or made to tidy their rooms or wear stupid clothes that they didn't want to wear. It was Jasper's favourite way of passing the time, and they'd been back in London incredibly quickly. That was one of the funny things about journeys. The journey there always seemed to take so much longer than the journey back. Tessa said it was because you were excited on the way there and every minute dragged because you were only thinking of arriving at your destination. But on the way back, you didn't want the journey to finish, so time went really fast.

Joy had been at Victoria station to meet them and

she'd dropped Jasper off at his home. It had been then that Jasper had been forced once again to think that Tessa didn't like him so much any more. He'd said he'd call for her next day as usual, so they could walk to school together, and she'd said, 'No, it's all right, I think I'll go in early. I said I'd meet Martin and Kamala to show them how to do the maths homework.'

'I don't mind going in early,' Jasper had said.

'No, it's all right,' Tessa had answered firmly, and with a sinking feeling, Jasper had taken the hint.

There were other signs, too, that Tessa was less interested in him now. Some dinner times she ran off to be with Martin, making it clear that she didn't want Jasper to follow. And sometimes, at home time, she would disappear before Jasper had even managed to gather up his things, and she'd be walking with Kamala and they'd be laughing and peering in shop windows at clothes and deciding what they would buy if they had the money to afford it.

Jasper gouged his desk with the point of his pencil, which snapped in two without making the slightest impression on the plastic table top. It was the diet that had changed Tessa, he decided. Now that she'd lost weight, she felt confident enough to look for other friends. He'd known from the start that the diet would be a mistake. He'd known that it would alter things.

'Jasper Woodrow, pay attention please.' Jasper turned slowly to face Miss Poole. He didn't see why he should pay attention. Nobody else did. Even Tessa didn't bother so much with her work any more. Now that she was getting thin, she didn't seem to think she needed to be clever too. In fact, she'd said that having brains was a positive disadvantage for a girl. It meant that you were called a swot and everyone was either scared of you or resented you. Jasper looked out of the window again. It seemed to him that this was a stupid attitude. People were jealous if you were clever but they couldn't admit to this, so they came up with some other reason for thinking it was wrong to be bright. If he, Jasper, could see through it, why couldn't Tessa?

'Jasper, I'm not telling you again. Pay attention.'

Jasper glanced at Tessa, who was sitting two desks away, hoping for a sympathetic grin or some other signal of solidarity. But she wasn't even looking at him, she was passing a note from Sonia to Martin.

Sonia. How could Tessa want to have anything to do with that girl after all the nasty things she'd said? It was beyond Jasper, it really was.

Jasper felt that Tessa was going the same way as the other vacuum heads in the class. She was playing about in lessons and giggling all the time about nothing. She only seemed to think about clothes now, and what was number one in the charts. She never used to be like that.

Jasper thought sadly that maybe it wasn't Tessa that was wrong; maybe it was him. If everyone liked those things, he was the odd one out, the freak. He hadn't minded being a freak when Tessa had shared the honour with him, but it was becoming harder now.

'Tessa,' he whispered, trying to catch her attention. 'Tess!'

The rest of the class sniggered and someone nudged Tessa, who turned warily in his direction.

He hastily scribbled a note: *Are you walking home with me tonight?* He passed it on.

The answer came back speedily: *No, I'm going to meet my mum.*

Jasper scribbled: *What for?*

The reply came even faster than before. *Mind your own bizzness.*

It was odd; Tessa was the best speller in the class. Now, suddenly, she couldn't even spell an easy word like business. What was going on?

Jasper decided to scrawl one last question for Tessa. *Am I still coming to your house for your birthday at the weekend?*

Tessa wrote back: *Of course you are, dummy, what do you think?* – leaving Jasper more confused than ever. Were they friends or weren't they? He really wasn't sure.

At ten o'clock on Saturday morning, Jasper banged on Tessa's door. Joy opened it and said, 'Come in, Jasper, she'll be down in a minute.'

Jasper waited patiently by the window, looking at the plants. There was a trailing ivy and a huge cheese plant that stood on the floor like a little tree.

'Hiya, Jasper,' Tessa said, and he turned to greet her. She wasn't alone. A Chinese girl, no taller than he was, came in behind her.

'This is Lucy. She's staying with me for the weekend.'

Jasper looked at Lucy. She was very thin and she had

straight black hair that was tied back with a long blue ribbon. She was wearing baggy jeans and a big bright green sweater. She smiled at him, and he smiled back, trying not to reveal his shyness by looking down before she did.

'Happy birthday, Tess,' said Jasper, holding out her present.

She pulled off the paper. It was a book about the West Indies, and Jasper had saved for ages to buy it. She flicked through the pages and then dropped it on to the sofa. 'Thanks,' she said. 'Lucy got me this T-shirt. It's great, isn't it?'

'It's nice,' said Jasper. 'What did your dad get you?'

As soon as he'd asked the question, Jasper wished he hadn't. It was clear from Tessa's face that no present from her dad had arrived as yet. 'I expect he's very busy,' said Jasper, and Tessa nodded. They slipped into an awkward silence.

Eventually, Jasper said, 'Are we still going out?' Whenever he went to see Tessa on Saturdays, they looked round the shops, browsing through CDs and books before having a snack lunch in a café. After that, if there was nothing good on television, they went to see a film. Jasper hardly ever had enough money for all this, so Tessa often paid, though he would bring things his mum had made so that he didn't feel so bad about it. Today, he had a large tin of homemade biscuits, which he offered to Tess.

She lifted the lid cautiously, as if she was afraid that something would jump out at her. 'You know I'm on a diet, Jasper,' she said.

'But you're nearly the right weight now.'

Tessa turned to Lucy with a look that said, 'This boy is clueless.' Then she said, in extra patient tones, 'Nearly isn't good enough. You'll have to take them home again or I'll just be tempted.'

'They're for your mum too.'

'Mum won't want them either. She's still trying to lose the weight she put on at Christmas.'

Jasper took back the tin and wondered how he was going to explain it to his mother. She might understand, but it was more likely that she'd be hurt in some way about it. He'd have to get rid of them somewhere. Only that was wasting food and money, and that wasn't all right either.

'What's the matter, Jasper?' asked Lucy in a concerned voice.

'Nothing,' he said. He didn't know her well enough to want to explain, and anyway, Tessa would have heard.

The shopping centre was a short bus ride from Tessa's house. They were lucky; a bus drew up at the stop just as they arrived. They ran upstairs, and Tessa grabbed the front seat, pulling Lucy down beside her. Jasper sat in the one behind.

'You see that building on the corner? That's our school.'

'It's big,' said Lucy.

'Too big,' said Tessa. 'I hated it at first, but I'm getting more used to it now.'

'My school's quite small.'

'You're lucky,' said Tessa and Jasper together.

'Before I got to know Tess, I didn't have any friends,' said Jasper.

Tessa looked embarrassed. 'I knew a lot of people but I didn't really want to be friends with them,' she said.

Jasper knew better than to point out the lack of truth in this.

'I've got lots of friends now,' Tessa added.

Jasper kept his attention on a wasp that was buzzing dementedly close to his ear. It wasn't really true that Tessa had a lot of friends now, either. It was more that the other kids didn't have so much to bully her about now that she was thinner, and that meant that she could at least sit with them and spend her breaks with them if she wanted to without them picking fights with her. Now that she had lost weight, she had become more like them, less the odd one out. And then she'd stopped snarling at people so much, so maybe now they were less afraid to get to know her. It didn't exactly amount to friendship with them though.

Jasper hit at the wasp with his bus ticket. The gesture was feeble and didn't stand a chance of working. The wasp continued to buzz near his ear, sounding even angrier than before. Tessa turned round and zapped it with a copy of a teen magazine. It dropped to the floor.

'You shouldn't have killed it,' said Jasper crossly. 'If you were a Buddhist, you wouldn't have been allowed to.'

'Well, I'm not a Buddhist, so it doesn't matter, does it?'

166

'It was still a living thing.'

'Well, so am I, and it's the survival of the fittest. It might have stung me.'

'If it was going to sting anyone it would have been me. It was my ear it was buzzing in.'

'You tried to kill it with your bus ticket.'

'No, I didn't. This bus ticket is about three centimetres wide and it doesn't weigh anything. How could I kill something with that?'

Tessa turned to Lucy and said, 'He's always going on about doing the right thing. He's so . . . good.' She wrinkled her nose, as though good was an extremely distasteful thing to be.

Lucy looked as if the argument wasn't happening, obviously not wanting to get involved. The bus pulled up outside Woolworths and they hurried off before they missed their stop.

Tessa took Lucy by the arm, leaving Jasper to follow behind them. They didn't head straight up the escalator and into the record shop as they usually did. Tessa went into the department store instead.

The first thing she and Lucy did was to try on lots of perfume. They sprayed the contents of the sample bottles on to their wrists which they then held to their noses and sniffed. It seemed to go on for ages, and Jasper didn't see how they could tell one scent from another by then. He wandered over to the men's range and tried to get interested in some aftershave, but the assistant looked at him as if he was the biggest joke ever, so Jasper wandered back to the perfume again, waiting for the others to get tired of the game. Luckily, they ran out of wrist space and went up to the next floor, with Jasper trailing behind. 'I wouldn't have dared to do that if I'd still been fat,' said Tessa to Lucy.

'Me neither,' Lucy replied.

'Did you see the sales assistants? They were all so thin.'

Lucy nodded. 'My grown-up cousin used to work here. She said they don't let you serve customers in the perfumery unless you're really pretty and slim like a model.'

Tessa silently assessed her chances of being allowed to work there when she was old enough. Before she'd begun the diet, she'd thought she might be a doctor, like her dad. Or maybe a chemist, like her mum. Something that required brains, anyhow, because brains were all she'd got. Now, a whole lot of glamour jobs were opening up. If she really tried hard enough to be wafer thin, she might even manage to be a model in years to come. It said in her magazine that some top models started at fourteen, if they were tall enough. She only had to wait two years.

Jasper listened to the conversation, wondering why being thin was so important that you couldn't even work in a shop unless you were. It made him miserable. He was never, ever going to look like other people, no matter if he went on a million diets or fattened himself up and worked out six hours at a stretch. He wondered what things in this world would be closed to him because of it, though he decided it probably wasn't so bad for boys. People always went on about girls being too fat or too thin or having short hair when it should be long. They were less fussy about what boys looked like, and once he was grown up, it probably would hardly matter at all.

The next stop was the hat department. This was even more boring than the perfume, because it went on for longer. Tessa put on a little boxy red hat that no one could possibly want to wear in a million years. It had a spotted black veil and looked really stupid, but Lucy and Tess thought it was very funny and almost cried with laughing.

Lucy tried a furry beret and it suited her. She said if she had the money, she'd buy it, probably. Tessa tried on a blue straw hat with a wide brim and it looked quite nice. Jasper, tired of standing and watching by himself, put on a yellow floppy hat, which he pulled down round his ears. Tessa and Lucy could hardly catch their breath, they were laughing so much, and Jasper brightened up too, pleased with himself for being part of things again.

'What's going on here?' A stern-looking man had come over and he was peering at them as if they were tiny insects at his feet.

They said nothing.

'This isn't a playground for children. Go on, get out, before I call security.'

Jasper slowly removed the hat. It was so mean, you couldn't even have a bit of fun any more. Tessa scowled, and Lucy looked frightened.

'We weren't doing any harm,' Tessa said as the man

followed them to the down escalator to make sure they were really going.

'Just get out of here, and don't come back. I'll remember you, don't you worry.'

Subdued now, they left the store. 'Well, what now?' said Tessa.

'Books?' asked Jasper, hopefully.

'No, we do that almost every Saturday. Anyway, Lucy doesn't want to.'

Jasper looked questioningly at Lucy, hoping that she might speak for herself, but she stayed silent. Tessa could be so bossy at times.

'Well, I want to go to the bookshop,' said Jasper, trying to stop the feeling that he was just Tessa's shadow and of very little importance.

'You can if you want, we're not stopping you.'

'Aren't you coming then?' said Jasper.

'No, I told you, we don't want to.'

Jasper wasn't sure what to do. If he didn't go to the bookshop, and went with them instead, he'd lose face. If he did, they would go somewhere without him, maybe for the rest of the afternoon. 'I could go and look at the books and meet you back here in ten minutes,' he said, thinking that this was the perfect compromise.

'We're going to look at some clothes,' Tessa said. 'We don't know how long we'll be, the changing-rooms are always packed on Saturdays. Tell you what, you go to see the books and if we've got time, we'll see you later in the coffee shop for milk shakes.'

170

'Not milk shakes,' said Lucy hurriedly. 'They make you fat.'

Jasper thought a milk shake was just what Lucy needed. Her knees and elbows were sharp and her legs were the width of one of his arms.

'What time will we meet up then?' he said.

'I don't know, I haven't got a watch.'

'It's quarter to twelve.'

'OK. Two o'clock then, if we're not doing anything else.'

'That's over two hours.'

'It takes a long time, trying on clothes.'

'What can I do for two hours?'

'I don't know, it's up to you.'

'Please, Tess –' Jasper began, and stopped himself. He wasn't going to beg her to be nice to him, he had more pride. He started to walk away. 'See you later, then,' he said.

'Maybe,' said Tessa.

Jasper thought that Lucy gave him a look which said she was sorry for pushing him out, but he couldn't be sure. As he headed for the bookshop, he knew there was no chance that they would meet him at two, but he planned to be there anyway, just in case.

18

Jasper had been right. Tessa hadn't turned up at the coffee shop. He'd sat there waiting for her for nearly an hour, not wanting to believe that she wasn't going to show. He kept looking towards the door, thinking once or twice that he saw her in the crowd outside. He wondered if the waitress had realized that he'd been let down. He'd been careful not to say that he was waiting for someone so that no one would feel sorry for him if he ended up stuck there on his own. He lingered on, making his glass of Coke last. Finally he sucked the dregs of it through a straw, paid the waitress and left.

All the way home he looked out for Tessa, half hoping to catch a glimpse of her, and half hoping he wouldn't. He wanted to tell her how angry he was that she could let him down like that and not even care. He wanted to shout and to scream, but he just wandered slowly towards home, walking because he'd spent his bus fare on the Coke.

He had hoped that his mother would be out when he got home, to save explanations, but she was in the living-room, watching a cricket match. 'I just have it on for the company,' she explained, as she saw him. 'I thought you'd be a long time yet. Why are you back so early?'

'We got fed up going round the shops,' said Jasper, trying to sound convincing.

172

'Have you quarrelled with Tessa?'

'No,' said Jasper, wishing that grown-ups didn't always jump to the conclusion that there'd been some sort of fight. If only it had been that simple. A fight he could have understood. All you had to do then was say you were sorry for whatever you'd done wrong. The other person then forgave you and you stayed friends. If he and Tessa had quarrelled, he'd know what to do to make things right.

'Something's bothering you, Jasper.'

'No, I'm all right.'

'Is that my biscuit tin? Give it here and I'll put it away.'

Jasper realized too late that he hadn't chucked its contents away as he'd intended. 'It's OK, Mum, I'll do it.'

'I'm going in the kitchen,' his mother said, stretching out her hand.

'Mum, Tessa's on a diet, she didn't want to eat the biscuits. Her mother was on a diet too.'

'What's she doing on a diet, a child of eleven?'

'She's twelve now.'

'Eleven, twelve, it's still too young. There's so much pressure on kids these days, it isn't right. Maybe she was a little plump. People are different shapes. Variety is interesting. We don't all look the same, the good Lord made us different. You know it makes me so mad. All this television: slim this, fit that, be this, do that. Why should women have to be like sticks, eh? There are times when I can't understand what's happening, you know?'

Jasper sat down beside her. There were times when he couldn't understand it either. 'Tessa thinks her father will come home if she gets thin enough.'

'Why would she think a silly thing like that? Her parents didn't split up because she was a little chubby, that's sheer foolishness.'

'Now that Tessa's getting thin, we're not such good friends.'

'Why not?'

'I think she wants to be with normal people.'

'What's all this normal, Jasper honey?'

'You know, people who look nice.'

His mother put her arm around him. 'You look nice, Jasper Woodrow, and don't ever let me hear you saying different.'

'I'm too short, Mum, and then there are my glasses. And it's going to be ages before my teeth straighten out.'

'Ever heard the Ugly Duckling story? There's a swan there, trying to get out.'

Jasper smiled. 'It's going to have a job.'

'Looks aren't everything. They're not anything, if you want my opinion. I'd rather have a kind, good-hearted, clever, sensitive boy like you any day of the week than some kid who thought he was God's most beautiful object.'

'You would say that.'

'Why?'

'Because you're my mother, and you're biased.'

'I say it because it's true.'

174

'If looks weren't everything, Mum, Tessa wouldn't have had to go on a diet, and she'd still be my friend, wouldn't she?'

'Sometimes you have to grow a lot before you know the worth of being kind, and true to yourself.'

'I don't think I understand what you mean.'

'You will, Jasper. Now give me that tin, and I'll fetch us some tea and we'll eat these biscuits.'

Tessa was feeling guilty. She knew she should have met Jasper at the coffee shop, but she'd wanted to have Lucy to herself. It was fun, going round the shops with another girl who liked the same things you liked. Jasper had been spoiling it. Tessa looked in the mirror in the bathroom. It had the best light; you could see whether you had any spots coming or not. So far so good. She went back into her bedroom.

It was Sunday evening, and Lucy had just gone. Tessa was missing her already. It was boring, being on her own again. She wondered if she should call Jasper and say she was sorry for not meeting him, but she hadn't promised absolutely that she would, she'd just said she might, so she didn't really need to apologize at all, she reasoned. After all, if Jasper was such a wimp that he had to follow her around all the time, that was his problem, wasn't it?

Tessa lay on her bed, and tried not to remember that she was Jasper's friend and that they'd had a lot of good times together. She also tried not to remember Jasper's kindness and his patience and the way he hardly ever said cross or spiteful things. But then that was the trouble with him, really. He was so good all the time, he was dull.

Tessa remembered her homework. She still hadn't done it and there wasn't much time left now. She went to her small desk and pulled her books out of a plastic bag they'd been languishing in since Friday. At the beginning of the school year, she'd done every bit of homework and tried to get it right, but there didn't seem to be so much point now that she'd decided to be something glamorous when she grew up. You didn't need GCSEs for modelling or being an actor, you only needed looks and talent.

'Tessa, have you done your homework yet?' called her mother.

'Nearly,' Tessa lied. She glanced at the title of her history essay. *Boring.* She scribbled a few hasty lines and moved on to maths. This held her attention more, but she couldn't be bothered to show her method of working out, it took too much time. French was OK, just writing what those stupid Marchands had been up to during their trip to the country – as if she cared. She scribbled the last sentence and shut her book with a bang. Then she put on her Walkman.

On her way to school next morning, Tessa met Martin. She liked him; he wore the right clothes and he was tall and slim, but not skinny. 'What did you get for the last problem in maths?' he asked.

'I don't remember,' said Tessa.

'Well, could you have a look? Only I got 847·825 and it doesn't look right.'

Tessa put her bag on the ground and fished out her maths book. The wind sent its pages fluttering. She smoothed them down impatiently. '820 exactly,' she said.

'How did you get that?'

'I don't remember,' said Tessa, 'but it is the right answer, definitely.'

'It's OK, I believe you. I'm useless at maths.' Martin crossed out his answer and put Tessa's in.

'Did you see *Big* at the weekend? It was on TV.'

'I saw it ages ago on video. It's quite good.' Tessa was flattered that Martin wanted to talk to her, but she wasn't going to seem too eager for his company. Besides, Sonia was coming over.

'Hiya Fatty,' Sonia said.

'I'm not fat,' Tessa replied.

'You'll always be Fatty to me, even if you fade to nothing. I've never had to go on a diet, I'm lucky, I'm naturally thin. It must be awful to have to watch what you're eating all the time. I'd hate it. And it's not as if the results are all that brilliant either. You've probably got stretch marks.'

Tessa didn't know what stretch marks were, but she found herself trying to remember how she'd looked the last time she'd seen her reflection in a mirror, in case any of the things Sonia was saying were true. Martin was just standing there, not saying anything. He was a bit of a coward really, and right under Sonia's thumb. Briefly, Tessa despised him for it. But he was nice-looking, and he did seem to like her now, so the moment passed.

Sonia went to talk to Kamala and Martin went with her, leaving Tessa standing by herself. Jasper was coming through the gate, so Tessa hurried over to the playing fields. She didn't want to talk to Jasper right now. He made her feel guilty, and that was annoying, so it was better just to ignore him.

It was almost the end of the summer term. Most of the tests were over, and Tessa didn't really care if she'd passed or not. Exams weren't important. Nothing was important except being thin. Lucy understood that. It was one of the reasons why Tessa liked being with her so much.

Tessa was looking forward to the holidays. Next term, everything would be different. She'd be really thin, for one thing, and people would have to like her then, and not just because she could do their maths homework for them. She imagined being transformed into the kind of person she'd always dreamed of being: beautiful, slender and loved. By the start of the next school year, it would almost certainly be a reality, as long as she could stick to the diet, as long as she didn't fall for the charm of a Mars bar or a sticky bun. She would do it . . . she had to do it. Everything depended on it.

19

Tessa stood in the changing-room. She held the pair of size ten jeans against herself and wondered if there was any chance at all that she was going to fit into them. She almost didn't want to try. It would be so disappointing if after all these weeks she was still the same fat ugly stupid person that she'd been before the diet.

She slipped off her skirt and pushed her feet through the legs. So far so good. She pulled the jeans up slowly and eased up the zip. She stared at the result in the mirror. A perfect fit.

It was true that they were cut in a baggy style – otherwise, she'd probably have needed a twelve, she decided. And her hips still seemed a bit wide, and her thighs were too big, that was for sure. But just the same, it was hard to believe that she'd actually done it, that she was standing there in size ten clothes.

She tried to decide if she actually wanted to spend the birthday money her father had finally sent on this pair of jeans. They had a teddy motif embroidered on the pocket (a bit childish) and when you rolled up the legs, a pretty cotton lining in pink and grey was revealed. But they fitted so well, they might have been made for her.

Tessa thought back to the time when her mother had bought her wedding outfit and they'd trailed round the shops, ending up in a changing-room not unlike this.

She'd been huge then, like a disgusting wobbling balloon. No wonder nobody had wanted to know her.

It was almost the end of the summer holidays and the time had passed slowly. Tessa had seen Jasper a few times, and they'd spent a week in Brighton with her father, but the trouble with holidays was that no one was around to notice what was happening to you. What would they think at school when they saw her in size ten clothes, completely unlike her old self? Even her hairstyle had changed, it was straighter and tied up in a bun with a wide strip of ribbon. She looked like a real, soft, sweet little girl.

The thought surprised her. She hadn't even considered the possibility. Before the diet, she had only thought of herself as fat, she hadn't thought about the way she looked in other senses. She stared at her reflection even harder than before. Yes, it was true, she looked cute, not tough or strong or anything. *Girly*.

Tessa wasn't sure how she felt about that. She'd never admired helpless girly girls, they had irritated her, however thin they had been. And here she was, joining their ranks. It was *weird*.

'Tessa, what are you doing in there?'

'Nothing, Mum.'

'Do you want those jeans or not?' called her mother from just outside the cubicle.

'Yes, I want them,' said Tessa, pulling them off and putting on her skirt again.

The purchase was made quickly. On the way out, Joy saw a pair of shorts in deep pink. 'I quite like these,' she said.

'They're a bit young, Mum,' said Tessa, embarrassed at the mere thought of being out with a mother who was wearing those.

'Not for me, silly, for you. They'd look nice on you.'

Tessa shook her head. She might be thin, but she wasn't ready in her head for such a big change as that. She was used to covering herself up and it would be a while before she felt confident enough to go around in skimpy clothes that didn't cover her thighs and barely covered her bottom. She hurried out of the store.

The first day of a new term always felt special – specially awful, usually, Tessa decided. But as she put on a set of completely new clothes, she felt high with anticipation. Things would be different now. She wouldn't be the most despised person in her class any more. Now she had style. Now, she was thin and likeable.

Tessa had told Jasper not to bother calling for her that morning. She wanted a new image, and being seen going into school with him would remind people of what she used to be.

'Are you ready yet, Tess?' said her mother, coming into the room.

'I've been ready for a good five minutes,' she answered crossly.

'Do you want a lift? What time's Jasper coming?'

'No, you go on without me, I've decided to walk.'

Joy put her arm round Tessa's waist. 'You look really nice. Are you sure you don't want to go in the car?'

'No, Mum, I like walking now. It's good for me.'

Even the walk to school seemed different. Tessa liked early autumn; the air was fresher but the sun still shone and the days had not yet shortened so much that you felt it was always dark. She liked kicking up leaves, and smelling smoke from bonfires and the way the trees were lots of different shades. She liked collecting conkers, though she wondered if maybe now she was twelve she ought to give it up. There was one lying on the ground just ahead, and she cracked it open with the heel of her foot. It was too soon though, there was just a seed inside, soft and not even brown as yet. Tessa threw it as hard as she could and watched it land in somebody's garden. Even her putting skills had improved.

She slowed down as she reached the school gates, unsure of herself for the first time. What if no one noticed how much weight she'd lost? What if they did?

She sauntered across the playground, trying to look confident. Janice said that confidence was part of being thin. You believed in yourself more. Tessa gave herself a mental shake. She was pleased she'd lost the weight, it was great, but she didn't have to believe all that mental rubbish they fed you. Her body was different, but she wasn't really a different person, was she? Apart from anything else, there were bits of her old self she'd quite liked and wouldn't have minded holding on to. This line of thought nearly stopped her in her tracks. It hadn't occurred to her before that she might have been OK as a person even when she was fat. She'd need some time to get her head round that one.

'Hello, Tessa.'

It was Jasper. Even the sight of him made Tessa uncomfortable. She'd hardly seen him in the holidays, and once, to her shame, she'd spotted him in the local library and had hurried out again as fast as she could. For an awful moment, she'd thought he'd seen her do it, but he didn't come after her or call out, so she decided she must have imagined it. It wasn't that she didn't like him any more. It was just that he was old news. She'd outgrown him, or out-slimmed him, to be more accurate. But she couldn't just ignore him when he was standing right there in front of her, so she said, 'Hello, Jasper,' but kept walking past towards Sonia and Martin.

'Well, look who it isn't,' said Sonia. 'My, aren't we looking wonderful with all that fat burnt off. Did you have liposuction then?'

'What's liposuction?' said Martin.

Tessa waited for the answer. She wasn't sure either.

'It's for mega fatties. What they do is, they stick a huge needle in and suck the fat out of you with a vacuum cleaner.'

'You're joking,' said Martin.

'No, I'm not, I saw it on telly. You can see she's had it done, she's full of holes.'

Martin laughed, and so did everyone else in earshot. 'I haven't had it,' said Tessa indignantly. Everybody laughed again.

'You know what? She has to go to this place where they make fat kids go on a diet.'

'I don't go there any more.'

'It's pathetic, isn't it? Old fat guts has to be taught how not to eat.'

Tessa felt a rush of anger. She wanted to slap Sonia in the mouth – that would shut her up. She moved forward, but felt a hand on her shoulder. Jasper was there. 'She's not worth it,' he said. Tessa turned round and marched off, still hearing the laughter as she went. 'Go away, Jasper,' she said. 'Leave me alone.'

Jasper shrugged and walked towards the school entrance as the bell summoned them inside.

As he walked down the corridor he smelled the usual odour of steaming socks and steak and kidney pudding. Only schools could combine this smell in such a distinctive way. Last year it had sent chills of terror rushing through him at the start of every term, but now there was an odd kind of comfort in the familiarity of it. There was sadness too. He'd been afraid that Tessa wouldn't want him any more and it was looking as if it was true. It had been her he'd seen hurrying out of the library, he was sure of it now, though at the time he had thought he might have been mistaken. Her weight loss had confused him. Her back view looked so different now. Her hair was longer and her outline was slim – even skinny. The curves that had marked her out before had gone and had been replaced by something that was strange to him. Tessa just wasn't the same. Maybe she'd never be the same again. The thought scared him so much that he broke out in a sweat. He was afraid of being alone again.

He trailed into the new classroom on the second floor. He saved a place for Tessa, but she walked straight past and sat in the row second from the back. Miss

Jenkins came in and said she was their new form teacher. He looked at Tessa to see if she was still minding about being made to wear lost property clothes one PE day, but she showed no sign. She was talking to Kamala who was sitting behind her.

Jasper wished that nice things could go on for ever and never have to change. Tessa had been all right as she was, why did she want to be like everybody else? He'd wanted her as his friend because she was different, and she'd seemed to like being different from everyone else. Well, he'd got that wrong, anyhow.

'Jasper, are you all right?' said Miss Jenkins.

Jasper nodded. 'I have a cold,' he said. He wiped his eyes with a strip of toilet paper and hoped that no one had seen it was a lie. No wonder Tessa didn't like him any more, he was a wimp, he cried in the middle of lessons about nothing. It was pathetic, it really was.

He focused on the classroom wall. The geography room was their form room that year and it was full of maps and charts. He picked out Jamaica, the tiny island on the right-hand side, and stared at it, willing himself to get tough. It would be all right. He'd be grown up in another six years and he'd get away from everyone and everything for ever and ever, only he'd send postcards to his mum because she'd worry about him however grown up he was. He'd send a postcard to Tessa too, because he'd want her to remember that once, long ago, they'd decided to go away together and to explore the island in a glass-bottomed boat.

20

The Tannoy system buzzed. Tessa removed her head-phones and waited for the announcement. 'Ladies and gentlemen, we regret our late arrival at Brighton Station. This was due to a points failure. We hope that it has not spoilt your journey and we apologize for any inconven-ience this may have caused.'

Tessa picked up her bag. If Jasper had been there, she would barely have noticed the extra hour spent waiting around. She wished she'd asked him now. No one at school need have known about it – Jasper wouldn't have told anyone. She'd thought of inviting Lucy, but when she'd phoned Mrs Szu had sounded really upset and had said that Lucy was ill in hospital. Tessa hadn't liked to ask what was wrong. Maybe on Monday she'd get Joy to ring up and find out for her.

As Tessa reached the ticket barrier, she realized that her father wasn't there to meet her. He'd probably got bored with waiting and gone off somewhere to pass the time. Tessa wondered if she could find her way to the flat on her own. She wasn't sure. Perhaps she ought to take a taxi. How much would it cost? She checked the money that Joy had given her in case of emergency. It would cover it, she was sure, but should she use it? And what if her dad was still somewhere in the station? He'd be furious if she just went off. Tessa remembered the time Paul hadn't been in and she and Jasper had gone to the park instead of waiting. Paul had really raged about that. She didn't want to risk it a second time.

She found a seat near their usual meeting place so that she'd see him if he turned up later. She began to read her magazine, but she'd gone through it twice already because of the lateness of the train. Come back Jasper Woodrow, all is forgiven, she thought with a sigh.

It was three weeks into term and she still hadn't impressed anybody yet. The other kids in her class hadn't changed their attitude to her all that much. The day before, she and Martin had been summoned by the new maths teacher, Mr Scott. She'd been a bit scared because he shouted a lot and was a sarcastic so-and-so, he really was. And he'd said, 'Can you tell me, Tessa, why you always seem to have the same answers as Martin, even down to the mistakes?'

Tessa wanted to say, 'Because he copies me,' but that would have been telling tales and it was up to Martin to say that anyway. Only Martin didn't say anything, he just stood there.

'You realize that neither of you will get any marks, either for this piece of work or for the two before that? What have you got to say for yourselves?'

Neither said anything, so Mr Scott ranted for a bit. 'You do realize that you have cheated? Cheating is stealing; stealing other people's work. And it is also a lie. Tessa, if you're too stupid to work on your own, you should come to me, not look over your shoulder at what Martin is doing.'

'But –'

'And Martin, you shouldn't give in to it. Allowing your work to be copied is just as stupid as copying itself.'

Martin looked embarrassed, but he still didn't admit that he was the one who'd done the copying. Tessa had been really angry. Why did Scott assume that she was the one who couldn't do it? Was it because she was a girl, or did he just like Martin better? Or was it because since last term her grades had been absolutely terrible? Tessa suddenly realized that Mr Scott had no way of knowing she was good at maths or anything else because she'd hardly done any work for ages. In the past, she wouldn't have made *any* mistakes in her work. It was the wrong answers that had given them away.

Still Martin had stayed silent, and when they'd been dismissed with two detentions each, he'd said, 'Thanks for not saying anything, Tess,' as if she'd done it because she liked him or something. And she didn't like him any more, not one bit, and she couldn't even think why she had ever liked him, she must have been off her head.

Something brushed Tessa's shoulder. She looked up. Her father was there, holding out a bag of doughnuts. 'Sorry, honey, I didn't realize the train had finally arrived. These will cheer you up.'

'Dad, I've told you so many times, I don't eat that stuff any more.'

'You must be hungry, though – it was a long journey.'

'I'm fine, Dad. Can't we just go back to the flat?'

He shrugged and picked up her bag. 'So you didn't change your mind about Jasper?'

'He's not my best friend any more. You can't have best friends who are boys.'

'Why not?'

'You can when you're a kid, but not when you're older. Jasper doesn't understand about clothes or anything. He's backward like that.'

'Last year, that seemed to be one of his charms. You were the one who was saying the girls in your class were shallow, only interested in clothes and makeup and who was going out with who.'

'I've grown up since then, Dad.'

Her father just smiled. 'Come on, let me at least buy you a salad. I haven't had time to shop.'

They went to a café in the Lanes that served lots of healthy food like yogurt and goat's milk cheese. Tessa tried to kid herself that she really enjoyed eating lettuce leaves and bean curd instead of Big Mac and fries. 'This isn't as slimming as you'd think,' she said.

'Isn't it?'

'It's dripping with salad dressing and dressings have oil in them. Oil's one of the most fattening things you can eat. *The* most fattening, probably.'

'Give yourself a break, Tess. Everyone's allowed a splurge every now and then. I hope you're not getting too obsessed with your weight. I've seen a lot of kids who've dieted themselves to nothing and have got real problems because of it.'

'No, Dad, I'm not obsessed, honest.'

'Make sure you keep it that way. How's school?'

'All right.'

'You don't sound sure, Tess. Are you still not happy there?'

Tessa concentrated on her salad. 'This year doesn't look like being much better than last year, to be honest.'

'If your mother and I could get you into another school, would that help?'

'Not really. It's just me, I don't fit in.' Tessa couldn't explain how disappointed she was that all the dieting hadn't made a difference to her friendships, she was almost as unpopular as ever. It was funny, every ad you ever saw on TV said that if you made yourself beautiful, everyone would want you. Maybe she just wasn't beautiful enough. Maybe she should still lose a few pounds, get her hair straightened, even try some working out with weights or whatever. Maybe that would help.

'Cheer up, Tessa.'

'Dad, do you think you'll be coming back home soon?'

She watched him carefully, trying to judge how truthfully he was going to answer her question. He seemed about to say something and then he got up and fetched another cup of coffee. He was putting off telling her, she could see that. It wasn't good news, then; it wouldn't be what she wanted to hear. As he returned to the table, she said, 'You're not coming back to live with us, are you, Dad?'

'No, Tess, I'm not.'

So it had all been for nothing then, all that self-denial.

It hadn't given her friends, and it hadn't brought her father back. It had been a complete waste of time.

'If I'd changed sooner, would you have come back then?'

'I don't know what you mean, Tessa. It's nothing to do with you; the way I feel about you is the same as it's always been. It's between your mother and me, it's nothing to do with anybody else. We told you that at the time of our separation. You said you understood that, Tess.'

You can understand things in your head, but it's still hard to believe them inside, Tessa thought to herself. She couldn't say it though; she felt too choked up.

'I know it's been hard for you, Tessa, and I'll make it up to you, I promise.'

'You're really sure you're not coming back? I mean, you won't change your mind or anything? It really is definite?'

'It's definite, Tess. We've decided to get a divorce.'

'Without telling me?'

'I'm telling you now, darling.'

'When was it decided?'

'Fairly recently.'

'It was Christmas, wasn't it?' said Tessa. She'd known then that it wouldn't be all right between her parents. They'd behaved as if they didn't know each other. There had been no real talking, and her dad had watched TV all the time to block everything else out. 'You should have told me. I had the right to know! Christmas was months ago, so you've known for ages and ages.'

'Not for sure.'

'Yes, for sure. If I knew, you must have known. I hate you!'

'Come on, Tessa, let's go home,' was all he said, and for the first time, Tessa realized that she had two homes, one in London, and one in Brighton. It was like she was split in half, not belonging to either, really, and always wanting the other home, whichever one she happened to be in.

21

Jasper was worried about Tessa. She hardly ever ate anything now, even though she was thin as a pin. Whenever he offered her something, especially if it was chocolate, she'd leap away like he was trying to poison her. He was learning not to do it, but it was hard to realize that Tessa didn't like food any more, and every now and then he forgot.

He was also trying to realize that Tessa wanted other friends. He alone wasn't enough for her now. At first, he'd been puzzled. Then he'd been angry, but that feeling hadn't lasted long, it had sort of worn itself out after two or three days. Then finally, he had accepted it. He couldn't make her like him as much as he liked her, and it was no good being cross about it, because that didn't change anything. The best thing to do was wait until Tessa realized that he was still her friend, and that would take a lot of patience. Jasper decided that he was lucky; he was a very patient sort of person. He wouldn't even have to work at it.

The last two periods on Tuesday afternoon were games this year. Jasper stood by as Sonia and Martin picked the people they wanted in their rounders teams. He was always the last one to be chosen because he was useless; he could barely see the ball, let alone catch it. He didn't mind, though, because he thought that games were a stupid waste of time. He'd rather be good at other things like English and science. They were a lot more useful than throwing a ball straight or being able to run.

He looked across at Tessa. Martin had picked her third, which was quite a compliment. Since she'd lost weight, she'd become a faster runner. Now, too, she concentrated more on what she was doing, which made her a useful person to have in a team. When she'd been fatter, she hadn't concentrated at all, and Jasper decided it was because she'd been too busy feeling awful about how she looked in her games kit.

'All right, Jasper, go and be with Martin. He can have an extra person in his team.'

Jasper went to stand with Tessa and the rest. They didn't look happy to have him, even as a sort of gift. Martin won the toss, which meant that his team would bat first.

'Don't run unless I tell you,' he said to Jasper.

'No, I won't,' Jasper answered, taking his place in the line after Tessa.

Jasper looked around him. It was quite a nice day, not too cold, and the sun came out from behind the clouds every so often and made him feel quite cheerful. He wished he hadn't ended up so far down the line of batters, though. The thought of having to face the bowler always made him nervous, and Kamala was good – even the best hitters didn't stand much of a chance with her.

It was his turn at last. Jasper just wanted to get it

over with. Then he could sit on the sidelines with the other useless ones until it was their turn to field.

Kamala did her usual graceful run up to the line, and then bowled. Jasper held up the bat, without really caring whether the ball hit it or not. To his surprise, there was a crack and the ball flew away from him.

'Run!' yelled Martin.

Jasper ran. Tessa was running ahead of him towards the second base. Jasper stopped at the first.

'Keep running!' shouted Martin, so Jasper went on, past the second base and on to the third.

'No, stop!' Tessa shouted. She could see she couldn't get to fourth without being stumped. Jasper looked at Martin, who was still saying 'Go!' so on Jasper went. Tessa was stumped out.

She turned to him. 'Fool!' she shouted. 'You never do anything right!'

Her words left Jasper raw. He stood at third base, wishing he hadn't run on like that. If he hadn't chosen to bat after Tessa, he couldn't have made her be out. 'But it's only a game,' he thought to himself, genuinely unable to see what all the fuss was about. So you scored a rounder or whatever they called it. So what? Tessa never used to care about things like that either, but now she did, it seemed. Jasper couldn't keep up with all the changes that Tessa seemed to be going through. She was like another person.

Jasper tried to get to fourth base but he didn't make it. He joined Tessa on the sidelines. 'Sorry I ran you out,' he said.

'It was stupid, you could see I couldn't get to fourth.'

'Martin said to run on.'

'Since when have you done what Martin said?'

'Since he was team captain. You're supposed to.'

'You're totally useless sometimes.'

Jasper was aware that his fingers had closed tightly round his bat. He was shaking. 'I am not useless,' he said quietly, but his voice trembled.

'Useless,' Tessa repeated.

Something inside Jasper blew. It was like a bomb going off inside him, and he could almost see the flash of light. 'Who do you think you are, Tessa Hislop? So you lost a bit of weight. It's made you ten times nastier than you ever were. You're stupid now, and boring, and you're just like everybody else.'

'Maybe I want to be like everybody else.'

'Well then, you're double stupid. They're dull as lead, and mean, and they move in packs. They don't even want you, but you don't care, you still want them. You humiliate yourself all the time, following that lot around. It's mad.'

'Well, you used to follow me around.'

'I can't think why. I won't be doing it any more, I can tell you that much.'

Jasper threw down his bat and began to walk inside. Miss Jenkins called after him, 'Jasper Woodrow, where do you think you're going?' but he kept on walking as if he didn't hear.

'Jasper!' called Tessa, frightened by his anger. He didn't even look back.

Tessa followed the others on to the pitch. It was their turn to field. Every now and then she looked up, hoping to see Jasper returning, but there was no sign of him. She wondered where he could have gone and what he could be doing. No one in her class had ever gone off like that before, and if she hadn't seen it for herself, she wouldn't have believed Jasper capable of it. He'd defied Miss Jenkins too, as if she didn't exist. It was strange behaviour, that was for sure, but somewhere inside of her, Tessa rather admired it.

She wished he hadn't said all those things about her, though. Was she really stupid? And boring? No, of course she wasn't, he'd just wanted to get back at her.

She watched as Sonia's bat connected with the ball and sent it soaring. Tessa ran back a little, jumped and caught it with one hand stretched high into the air.

'*Excellent!*' shouted Martin.

Tessa grinned. Then she remembered the trouble over the maths homework. Did it really matter what Martin thought of her any more? But it was very satisfying to have caught Sonia out. It was one of those really special moments that you replayed over and over in your head for the sheer joy of it. Tessa concentrated hard, trying to recapture the exact expression on Sonia's face when she'd realized what had happened, and that Tessa had been the one to vanquish her. And vanquish was the right word, because with Sonia everything was a fight, whether you wanted it to be or not.

The game was almost over now, and Tessa was relieved. She was much fitter than she used to be, but she felt weak and her legs weren't steady. She wondered if maybe she should have eaten more lunch, but she'd eaten a potato, some carrots and two apples as it was.

The whistle blew and Tessa collected the balls and carried them inside.

'Think you're clever, don't you?' said Sonia.

'You're just a sore loser.'

'Not as sore as your little boyfriend, wherever he's gone off to.'

Tessa sighed. In the excitement of the catch, she'd almost forgotten Jasper and the guilty feelings he'd stirred in her. She knew she hadn't been fair to him, but she couldn't help it, she wanted to belong more, and not just to a club for misfits. If he had any sense, he'd try to fit more too, because it made life so much easier. Or at least, that was the theory. Tessa was tired. Her life wasn't easier at all right now, it was getting harder all the time, and if there was one thing she really wanted, it was a Mars bar, but she'd die before she'd eat one. She still had to get a whole lot thinner. Maybe then she'd have friends, and maybe then her dad would like her enough to come back home.

22

'Mum, if you were really worried about someone because you knew they were doing something that was wrong, what would you do?'

Jasper's mother poured more milk into her coffee and added a couple of spoonfuls of sugar. 'Who are you talking about, Jas? Is it Tessa?'

'I'm not naming names, it wouldn't be right.'

'Well, what sort of trouble is she in? Stealing? Cutting school? What?'

'No, it's not that sort of trouble. In a way, it's worse.'

'Worse?'

'More serious.'

Jasper's mother looked worried. What could be more serious than the suggestions she'd already come up with? 'You'd better tell me what it is then.'

'I can't. She'd never forgive me. We had a quarrel yesterday – a really big one – and I don't know if we can ever get back to the way we were. If I tell on her, there won't be any chance at all.'

'Sometimes, the only way to help someone is to "tell on them", as you would put it.'

'That's the kind of thing grown-ups always say.'

She laughed. 'Perhaps that's because we've seen a bit more of life than you have.'

'I can't win then, can I? Grown-ups are always going

to be right just because they're old and it doesn't matter what I think.'

'You know that's not what I mean, Jasper. Look, hon, if you want advice, you have to give me a bit more to go on.'

'Do you promise you won't tell anyone then?'

'How can I promise that before I know what you're going to tell me? The most I can say is that I won't tell anyone without telling you I'm going to tell them first. How's that?'

'Not OK.'

'Not?'

Jasper shook his head vigorously.

'Then I don't see how you're going to help your friend.'

'I don't think I do either.'

'Try. Is she in trouble at home? Is something going on there?'

'Not really. Well, sort of, but it's going on at school as well.'

'So it's not that she's being bullied.'

'No.'

'And it's not that she's got a boyfriend or someone apart from you?'

'I'm not her boyfriend. No one is.'

'Jasper, I can't play twenty questions like this, it'll take all afternoon. Just come out with it. Take a chance that I won't make things worse. Come on, you can't really believe I'll do that, or you wouldn't be trying to tell me in the first place.'

200

Jasper didn't speak for a while. He was trying to weigh up the possible consequences. In the end, he said, 'It's her diet, Mum.'

'Oh. She's not eating enough?'

'Not nearly.'

'Skipping dinner?'

'Skipping almost everything. She's getting thinner and thinner, Mum. You know *Lord of the Rings*?'

'I haven't read it.'

'Well, anyone who wants the ring, the ring that makes you really powerful, gets taken over by it, and they can't think of anything else, and they fade before your very eyes until they become a ring wraith, a kind of shadow, and they're really unhappy and sort of trapped. That's what's happening to . . . my friend.'

'What are her parents doing about it?'

'I don't think they're doing anything. Her dad's not there any more, and they're getting a divorce, it's definite now. Tessa's really upset about that. Her mum thought the diet was a really good idea, so I don't think she'd mind how much weight she lost. She thinks being thin is great.'

'Maybe for herself, but it's not something you really want for kids. How much weight has Tessa lost? It's ages since I've seen her.'

Jasper realized he must have said her name. Oh well, his mum had guessed anyway. 'She's very, very thin, Mum. I mean, less than half the size she was.'

'I expect the teachers have noticed, Jas.'

'They just think she's gone on an ordinary diet.'

'But that's not what you think.'

'She's starving herself. And making herself sick if she thinks she's eaten too much.'

'Are you sure about that? The sick part, I mean?'

'Totally sure.'

'How do you know?'

'I just do. So you see, it really is bad, Mum. And her friend, Lucy, she's already in hospital because she's been doing it too.'

'And you think Tessa's going the same way?'

'She is. Definitely. And no one's doing anything to stop it.'

'OK, Jasper, don't worry. I'll talk to Tessa's mum.'

'And you'll make her see it's more than just a diet now?'

'Yes, I will.'

'And you'll tell her not to let on to Tessa that it was me who told on her?'

'Jasper, you haven't "told" on her. My guess is that you've helped her a lot. Just leave it to me, love. It'll be sorted out.'

Tessa slammed the front gate behind her. It had been a terrible day. She'd got low grades for everything and no one had spoken to her much. Martin had smiled at her, and at morning break he'd said how good it was that she'd got Sonia out in that rounders game the other day because Sonia was getting way too big for her boots. But Tessa didn't even like Martin any more, she hadn't done for ages, and if she was getting the better of Sonia, it was for her own sake she was doing it, not his.

She was still feeling guilty about Jasper too. She'd never meant to stop being friends with him completely, it had just sort of happened. She'd hoped that if she saw less of him, it would make her look better in the eyes of the other kids, but it hadn't been like that. Now, instead of having lots of other friends, she didn't really have anyone. It wasn't fair. Wasn't being thin supposed to change your whole life? That's what Janice and Bill had said. So she could get into size ten jeans. In fact, she could now get into size eight jeans. So what? Being fat hadn't been any fun, but being thin wasn't a whole lot of fun either, and at least she'd been her own person when she was fat. She didn't know who she was any more, and that was scary.

Tessa opened the front door and stopped still. She could hear her father's voice coming from the kitchen. She ran towards him. 'Dad! You've come home!'

'I'm just on a visit, Tessa darling,' he said, and she pulled away from him, disappointed. Still, at least he was there, and he had come all the way from Brighton. That had to count for something.

'Sit down, Tess,' said Joy.

Tessa sat, her suspicions aroused by her mother's firmness and the worry that was in her eyes. Something was happening. 'What are you doing here, Dad?'

'Tessa, we're worried about you. You're getting so thin,' he said.

Tessa remembered what Sonia had said months and months ago. 'You can't be too rich or too thin,' she repeated out loud.

Joy smiled and said, 'I've never rated having loads of money. It makes you mean.'

'You rate being thin though, don't you? I mean, you're always on a diet, and you're no bigger than I am.'

'I'm a lot bigger than you are, Tess. That's one of the things that worries me. You don't seem to see how thin you've got.'

'Well, you wanted me to get thin. It's no use complaining now.'

'I wanted you to be happier, and you seemed miserable carrying all that weight.'

'I was miserable because everyone treated me like I was nobody because I was fat. And that includes you.'

'Now that's not fair, Tessa.'

'Oh, yes, it is.'

'Tessa, don't start blaming your mother. She only wanted the best for you.'

'Why shouldn't I blame her? You blame her for everything all the time. You blamed her because the house wasn't clean enough and for being too busy to do things for you. And you blamed her for being out a lot because of her studying. And you blamed her for –'

'Tessa!'

'Well, you did.'

Tessa intercepted the look that passed between her parents. They seemed shocked by what she was saying, and kind of afraid.

'We're not here to talk about that now, Tess. It's you we're worried about.'

'That's right, push it back on to me all the time.'

'We're not, love,' said Joy.

'Tess, you can't go on the way you're doing. I mean, look at you. You're starting to look ill.'

'I'm OK.'

'You're not OK, and it has to stop.'

'I'm not getting fat again.'

Paul took her hand. 'I'm not asking you to get fat. Just to start eating proper meals.'

'I do.'

'You don't,' said Joy. 'I can't remember the last time we ate a full meal together.'

'I eat at school.'

'That's not what Jas . . .'

'You've spoken to Jasper?'

'No, not exactly, Tess.'

'It's him, isn't it? He's been saying things about my eating.'

'It's not like that —'

'Interfering little pig! I could kill him for this. It's not even true. He's just trying to get back at me for not being his friend any more. I hate him!'

'Jasper cares about you. He cares a lot more than any new friends you may have made,' said Paul.

Tessa began to cry. 'It's not fair! You're all against me now.'

'That's not true, love,' said Joy.

'You won't let me be fat, and you won't let me be thin.'

'Tessa, come on,' said Paul.

'It's true!'

205

'It's not true. Tessa, listen to me for a minute. You remember Lucy?'

Tessa shook her head, though she did remember. Lucy was in hospital being made to eat, because she had got so thin that her mum and dad were afraid she was going to die.

'If you carry on the way you are, you'll end up in that sort of state too. I see it all the time on the wards, kids getting messed up by wanting to be thin so much it's all they can think about. And it's also a way of getting attention from people, Tess, which makes your mum and me think that you must be pretty unhappy right now, and upset about what's happening with the divorce and everything.'

'It's got nothing to do with that.'

'I'm sorry that what's been happening has been so difficult for you. We've all got to try harder, you, me and your mum, to sort things out.'

'Does that mean you're coming home?'

Paul shook his head. 'But it does mean I'm going to be around a lot more, OK?'

Tessa nodded. 'OK.'

'But part of the bargain is that you start eating regular meals. Is it a deal?'

'Maybe.'

'Is it or isn't it, Tess?'

'I have to think about it,' Tessa said.

23

Tessa walked along the corridor. She was sorry now that she'd ever agreed to see Lucy; it was a great, big, ginormous mistake. She didn't like hospitals, she hated them. And this wasn't even like a normal ward; the patients were dressed in ordinary clothes, not pyjamas, and they were walking about as if there was nothing wrong with them. It was confusing.

It was hard to believe that Lucy had been there for so long. It was more than a month since Tessa had spoken to her mother on the phone, which meant that Lucy must have been in hospital for six weeks or more. Tessa had meant to visit sooner, but she'd kept putting it off. The idea that there was something wrong with being thin was scary. Everything became all right when you lost weight, and the more weight you lost, the better life got . . . didn't it?

Tessa felt guilty too. She'd known that Lucy had more or less stopped eating, but she hadn't done anything about it. She'd thought it was good. She'd actually felt envious and she'd wished that she could stop eating completely too. That kind of will-power had seemed brilliant, something to die for. And there was another thing that was niggling away at Tessa. It worried her whenever she thought of it. Lucy had taught her the most wonderful trick. On days when you just had to eat a cream bun or a Mars bar, you could make everything right by sticking your fingers down your throat and being sick. It was called having your cake and eating it, and it was the best idea ever. Or at least, she'd thought it was. But what if it made you ill? What if she wound up in hospital too? She wanted to run off the ward but she didn't. Instead she went up to a nurse and asked where Lucy was.

The nurse directed Tessa to the day room. Lucy was there, watching television. 'Hiya,' said Tessa, relieved that Lucy didn't look all that different from usual, though she was very thin.

'Hiya,' said Lucy, but she kept her eyes on the TV screen.

Tessa stood in the doorway, wondering what she should do. Lucy hadn't asked her to sit down, and she didn't seem that pleased to see her. 'Is it OK if I sit here for a bit?' Tessa asked at last.

'If you want to.'

Tessa sat on the edge of a well-worn sofa. 'I didn't expect it to be like this.'

'Like what?'

'You know, no beds.'

'There are beds. There are dormitories at the other end.'

'Yes, but everything seems . . .'

'Normal?'

Tessa smiled. She was embarrassed. 'How are you feeling?'

'Fine.'

Now that Tessa was closer to Lucy, she could see that she didn't look fine at all. It was partly her weight – she looked so thin it was . . . ugly. Tessa thought about the word. How could being thin make someone look less pretty than they'd been before? Being thin meant being beautiful, didn't it? Lucy didn't look beautiful though. She just looked ill, with her bones sticking out all over the place. But it was more than that. She looked as if something was hurting her, but not something in her body, something in her head. She looked the way Tessa looked when her parents were arguing, or when Sonia was being cruel.

'Why are you staring at me?' said Lucy.

'Sorry. I didn't mean to.'

'It's because I'm fat again, isn't it?'

'But you're not.'

'They've made me put on six kilos since I've been here and they say I've got to put on another ten at least before they'll let me go home.'

'That's because you got so thin.'

'I wish I still was.' Lucy still wasn't looking at Tessa.

'But you are.'

'I'm not, I'm gross.'

Tessa started laughing.

'See? You're laughing at me.'

'No, I'm not. I'm laughing because you're so thin, but you still think you're fat. It doesn't make sense.'

'I hate myself.'

'Why?'

'Because I've got fat again.'

'You haven't, Lucy, honestly,' said Tessa. She couldn't understand why Lucy didn't see how frighteningly thin she looked.

A girl who seemed to be a year or two older than Lucy came and sat opposite. Tessa tried not to stare at her but she couldn't help it. This girl was the thinnest person she had ever seen. It was hard to figure out how her legs could carry her. They were pencil thin and looked as if they would snap under the slightest pressure.

'That's Geraldine,' said Lucy in a whisper. 'She's my friend here.'

'She doesn't look very well,' Tessa whispered back.

'She's a lot thinner than me. It isn't fair. I wish I was still as thin as that.'

Tessa glanced at Geraldine again and thought it was strange of Lucy to want to look like that. 'Is everybody here because they don't eat?' she asked.

'Everybody on this ward.'

'How many are there?'

'Fifteen, I think.'

Tessa hadn't meant that, she'd meant how many people are there in the world who want to be thin so much that they land up in hospital? She felt in her pocket for her sugar-free mints and offered them round. Then she said, 'I don't see why people can't be all different sizes. When you think about it, I mean, *really* think about it, what's so terrible about being fat?'

'It is terrible.'

Tessa knew what she meant. In some ways, it was

terrible, or at least, people made you think it was. 'But *why* is it terrible?' she said. She was asking herself the question as much as she was asking Lucy.

'Nobody likes people who are fat.'

Tessa thought about it. Then she said, 'I had a friend when I was fat. I don't have any friends now. And what about you? I shouldn't think you've made many friends. You've spent most of the time since you've been thin in hospital.'

'It is terrible to be fat,' Lucy insisted. 'I know it is.'

'No, you're wrong,' answered Tessa. 'I thought that too, for a while, but at least when I was fat I was a real, living, breathing person. At least I knew how I felt about things, and at least I was really me. I don't feel like me any more, I feel like . . . I don't know. Like I'm what other people want, not what I want. I don't know how to explain it better.'

Tessa wound down and thought about what she'd just said. She hadn't known she felt like that until the words had come out. It was odd. She'd always thought she'd like herself better if she was thin, but it was becoming more and more obvious that she didn't like herself any better at all. So where did that leave her? What was she supposed to do now if being thin didn't make her feel all right? She wanted to cry but she knew she mustn't. She'd come to cheer Lucy up, not to make things worse. Lucy was her friend because Lucy understood what it was like to be fat, and what it was like to get thin. But maybe they'd both got it wrong, maybe it was different from what they had expected. Maybe being thin wasn't the answer to everything.

'Are you all right, Tessa?' said Lucy.

Tessa nodded. 'I'm sorry,' she said.

'What are you sorry about? It's not your fault.'

'It is, kind of. I helped you to stop eating.'

'No, I did that by myself.'

'I didn't really notice. I mean, I didn't notice you were getting ill. How long has it been since you stopped eating properly?'

'A long time. I didn't think I was losing weight quickly enough on the diet, so I speeded things up by eating even less than I was meant to eat. Some days I only had fruit and a couple of packets of crisps. No one noticed. My mum and dad work downstairs in the shop most evenings so I usually get my own meals.'

'It's easier to lose weight when no one's watching you,' said Tessa.

Lucy nodded. 'Everyone was so pleased with me when I lost all those pounds. Bill and Janice thought it was amazing, it was like I was proving what a good job they were doing with the club and everything. When I got to my target weight I still felt I could do better, that I wasn't as thin as I ought to be, so I carried on eating as little as possible all the time. It was such a good feeling, it was as if I was stronger than anybody and I could do anything I wanted. I don't just mean not eating, I mean it was as if I was stronger with other things too, because I had more will-power than other people, which meant I was better. Do you know what I mean?'

Tessa nodded. She'd started to have those feelings too.

'Some days, I didn't eat at all, but I made people think I'd eaten a lot. You get good at hiding things. I wore baggy clothes in case people thought I was losing too much weight too quickly. It worked. No one knew for a very long time.' Lucy put her fingers in her mouth and started sucking them as if she was a baby. Then she said, 'You know, Tessa, what I really wish is that everything could get back to normal.'

'Me too,' said Tessa, with a long sigh. 'Me too.' She stood up.

'You're not going, are you?' asked Lucy in a panicky voice.

'I can't stay. I told my mum I'd only be out for an hour or so.' Tessa looked guilty. She hadn't told her mother any such thing, she just wanted to get away, to think about everything on her own for a while.

'Please stay, Tess. You understand about this. I can talk to you.'

Tessa slowly sat down again. You couldn't just walk out when you were somebody's friend, it wasn't fair. And maybe she did understand. Maybe she understood well enough to be the one person who could show Lucy that being thin had its drawbacks.

It was long after tea-time when Tessa got home. She'd watched Lucy eat the huge meal the nurses had given her. It was horrible, being in hospital, much worse than school. Tessa had made up her mind that whatever happened, she wouldn't let herself get into such a state. It wasn't worth it.

Being at the hospital had made Tessa think of Jasper more than she'd done in ages. He'd seen what was happening to her with the diet and he'd tried to stop it. Maybe he'd gone about it the wrong way, telling his mum and all that, but he'd tried to be a friend, which was more than she had been for Lucy.

Tessa switched on the television and tried to stop thinking for a while, but the thoughts kept coming anyhow. She remembered the fun she and Jasper used to have when they visited her dad. And she remembered all the games they'd played and the things they'd shared that no one else would ever know about. She missed him. How could she miss stupid old Jasper? He was just a kid, he hadn't grown up at all, probably never would. But maybe that was it. He wasn't grown up, so he didn't pretend about anything. You could rely on Jasper.

Tessa sighed and stretched out on the sofa. She was suddenly aware of her thin arms and slender legs. It was as if her body didn't belong to her any more. She wasn't herself, she was somebody else, and she was tired of it. Jasper had liked her for what she was, and that had meant something. Why hadn't she been able to do the same for him?

Tessa went to the phone and picked it up. Then she put it down again. Maybe he'd tell her to get lost. She deserved it, but it would be such a climb-down to try to make up and then find he didn't want to know her any more. She began to watch TV again. Some puppet was being interviewed as if it was a real person. People were crazy, they'd try to get you to believe anything. Tessa switched it off. What if she asked Jasper if she could come over for a while? It wouldn't have to be a big deal, she could say it like she didn't care whether he said yes or not. Tessa picked up the phone again and dialled the number. Jasper's mother answered. 'Is Jasper there?' said Tessa, in her coolest voice.

24

Jasper was looking out of the window. Yesterday evening, Tessa had phoned him and said, with great casualness, 'I might come round to your place tomorrow. Are you going to be home?'

Jasper had only nodded, forgetting that Tessa couldn't see him. 'Are you still there?' she'd asked crossly. 'Yes,' Jasper had replied, meaning both that he was still there and that she could come round. He hadn't been able to figure out what was going on. Tessa hadn't spoken to him for weeks, and now suddenly she was talking about dropping round like it was no big deal at all.

She hadn't said she was definitely coming. Maybe she wouldn't. Maybe it was all just a wind-up to spite him for telling on her about the diet.

Jasper heard a noise outside the front door. He opened it eagerly, but it was only his mother coming home from work. 'Take the bags into the kitchen, will you, Jas?'

'I need to see out of the window. You can't from the kitchen.'

'Just take them, Jasper, and don't argue.'

He hurried in with the bags and dumped them on the kitchen table.

'Don't just leave them like that. I've been out at work all day, I could use a little help.'

Jasper unpacked flour, biscuits, tea, coffee and

oranges. He put two cartons of milk in the fridge, and also a packet of minced lamb. Then he hurried back to the window.

'Sitting by the window won't make any difference. You know what they say: "A watched kettle never boils."'

'It's a stupid expression. Kettles boil whether you watch them or not.'

'But they don't boil any quicker, do they?'

'I don't think she's coming. It's getting late.'

'It's not that late. I'm glad you two have patched things up.'

'But we haven't, Mum, that's the trouble. I don't know why she's coming, or even if she's coming. I don't know anything at all.'

'Don't get all wound up, just be patient. You used to be such a patient boy.'

'Patience is boring,' Jasper said.

The doorbell rang. Jasper jumped.

'Aren't you going to answer it then?'

'You get it, Mum.'

'Not on your life. Answer that door, Jasper Woodrow.'

He opened it slowly. Tessa was standing there. She was smiling at him. 'About time too. I haven't got all night, you know. Can't I come in?'

'If you want.'

Tessa said, 'Hiya, Mrs Woodrow.'

'Nice to see you, darling. Why don't you and Jasper go on to his room? I'm sure you have a lot to talk about. I'll fetch you some orange juice, OK?'

'Thanks, Mum,' said Jasper.

Tessa was still playing it cool. She stood in Jasper's room as if she wasn't sure whether she was going to stay or not. Jasper was looking nervous. He was standing by the window rolling an old Corgi car across the ledge. He looked about six years old and he made Tessa smile. It was good to be there again, she decided, but she wasn't going to let it show. The room felt different though, not like she remembered it. Tessa looked around, trying to work it out. Then she noticed that all the maps had gone. 'Why have you taken everything off the walls?' she asked in surprise.

'There didn't seem much point in keeping it all,' Jasper answered. He didn't say he'd taken everything down because he'd given up believing Tessa would ever go away with him, but she knew it anyway.

She came further into the room and sat on the bed. She'd spoilt things for him. The idea made her cross. She was tired of feeling guilty. First it was Lucy, and now Jasper. It was so complicated, being friends with people. She'd thought you just liked someone and they liked you back, she hadn't understood how messy it could get. 'You didn't throw the maps out, did you?' she asked.

'No,' said Jasper, surprised that Tessa was speaking to him kindly. He'd been expecting her to make fun of him. 'I've still got all the maps,' he said. He hadn't actually been able to bring himself to throw any out, although he'd felt stupid for holding on to them.

Tessa slid to the floor. 'Go and get them then, I want to have a look at them. It's ages since we've done this.'

Jasper opened several drawers and eventually all the maps were lined up in front of them.

They remembered all the journeys they used to plan and even found a few more. Tessa said, 'I want to go to Halfway Tree. It's such a good name for a place, isn't it? I've heard my dad talk about it. Don't your grandparents live near there?'

Jasper shook his head. His grandparents had left Jamaica a few weeks back and were now living with his uncle in Chicago. It would be great to visit them there. He mentioned this hesitantly, thinking that Tessa would say it was a stupid idea.

She didn't, though. She nodded and said, 'It's not that far to America from Jamaica. And they've got wonderful doughnuts there with lots of different fillings, and all sorts of flavours of popcorn. Did you know that over there, you can get melon and pizza and apple flavour? And they do great ice cream, too, really massive sundaes.'

It was good to hear Tessa talking about food again. It reminded Jasper of how things used to be.

'And you know what else they've got? Theme parks. Disney World, and loads of others, really brilliant ones. You can ride all day, it's just amazing. We could visit every single theme park. We could go on that roller-coaster ride, the biggest one in the whole world.'

'I'd like to see New York,' said Jasper. 'I'd like to ride the subway and see Maceys and the Empire State Building.'

'We could go all over. We could do California too, and try surfing. I bet I could surf.'

219

'I bet I could too. When I grow up, I'm going to be good at sports.'

'Why? It doesn't matter if you are or not, Jas. Anyway, I like you the way you are.'

'Do you, Tess?'

'You bet I do.'

His mother came in then, with two large glasses of orange juice and a plate of thickly sliced cake.

Tessa reached for the largest piece, and began to eat it with her old enthusiasm.

'Leave some for me, then,' said Jasper.

'You'll have to be quick if you want to keep up with me,' Tessa answered.

Jasper thought about it. He was quick now, and getting quicker all the time. He'd keep up with Tess all right. 'No problem,' he said with a grin, and he reached for his share of cake.